Flawed and All

Shekia Mason/Ni'Kay Rountree

This book is a work of fiction. All of the characters, organizations, and events portrayed in this novel are either products of the authors' imagination or are used fictitiously.

DEDICATION

To my pen sister, Nikki: It was an honor and a privilege to pen this story with you. You pushed me creatively and made me work when I didn't feel like it. I promise you that you inspire me every day and I look forward to all the years of friendship and sisterhood in our future. The best is yet to come! Thank you! Thank you! Thank you! To our readers and supporters, there are not enough words for us to thank you guys! Everything we do is for you! Hope you all enjoy this read!

Prologue

What's up? I'm Yvette. Not the type of chick that most would consider a "bad bitch". I'm five-five, dark skinned with plain eyes and what yall would consider short, nappy hair. And even though I have a big ass, I still have an average body. Honestly, I've always seen myself as that one ugly friend among my girls. I'm definitely a plain Jane. No Gucci, Fendi, Prada. No Michael Kors bags. No fancy cars. Nothing.

But none of that matters now, because today is my wedding day and I will be marrying the love of my life, Corey. Trust me, getting here wasn't easy. I put up with a lot of bullshit and fought hard to get and keep my man.

Corey is a Morris Chestnut looking type of guy. He stands an even six feet tall with gorgeous brown eyes, a cocoa complexion, and muscular frame. And he was a big time hustler. A legend in the Houston, Texas streets. Money and good looks draw women like flies to honey and Corey had both. That's why I couldn't believe I had been lucky enough to pull him. Never in my wildest dreams would I have ever imagined that Corey would be my boyfriend, let alone that I would be marrying him.

I met him at a nightclub a while back. From the moment I laid eyes on him, something about him just drew me in. The vibe I got when he looked my way made me believe in love at first sight. I stared at him from a distance because I knew he was out of my league. A fine ass brother like that would never date a frumpy chick like me so I didn't make a move, just sat at a table, sipped my drink and stared. After a few shots of liquid courage, I let my friend Candace convince me to approach him. And that's when this all began.

Yvette

I looked at my iPhone for the hundredth time. It was ten o'clock on a Friday night and I was sitting at home… alone… again. I had been waiting for my boyfriend, Shawn to come home. We were supposed to be going out for dinner and a movie. I was mad as hell. Shawn and I had been together about two years and he'd been doing this same shit for at least a year and a half of that time. I tried to leave him over and over, but every time I built my nerve to do it, Shawn would beg me to stay. It was hard for me not to take him back. I was twenty-four years old and he was my first real boyfriend. I wasn't the most attractive chick on the block and Shawn always reminded me of that. So I always stayed. He'd straighten up for a month or so, then go back to doing the same old things.

Tonight was no different than any of the other nights he left me alone. Except this time, I was truly fed up. He wasn't answering his phone or returning any of my text messages. So I decided if Shawn didn't do me right, another man would. It was time for me to get my black ass off the couch and have some fun. I called my girl, Candace. She was young, single and always in the mix so I knew she would be down to come through and swoop me up.

Candace ditched me for the dance floor the moment we walked past security. That's how she was, a real club rat. I had to admit it was packed wall to wall and popping. People were swarming around the building like ants preparing for winter, but I spotted him anyway. All six feet of him. I sat staring at him and sipping my drink until he

4

finally looked my way and caught me staring. I tried to turn away but couldn't. The moment we locked eyes he was the only person I saw. I froze under his gaze. He smiled. My heart beat a little faster. My palms started to sweat. I nearly pee'd my pants when he motioned with his index finger for me to come over. I looked down at the slut fit I was wearing. I'd let Candace choose my attire. She told me I needed to step my game up if I was going to pull a man besides Shawn's mediocre ass. So here I was in a black halter crop top two-piece dress. Both the top and bottom pieces had sheer mesh cut outs so I was showing plenty of skin. I wasn't comfortable but Candace convinced me I looked good. I stood up to go toward him, but had my work cut out because the skirt was skin tight and I wasn't used to walking in four inch stilettos. That again, was Candace's idea.

As I got closer, Corey's smiled widened. Then something inside told me to look back. That's when I saw her. There was a beautiful woman on my trail. She was headed toward Corey, too. She was Beyoncé fine, so I was no competition. He had been gazing at her behind me the entire time. My heart shattered into a million small pieces. I was embarrassed beyond belief. I didn't know what else to do besides tuck my tail and go back to my table. So that's what I did.

I watched from afar as she invaded his personal space. They talked for a few minutes before making their way to the dance floor. I couldn't stop watching them. She gyrated her body all against his. It was torture to watch, but I kept right on looking until Candace came back to the table for a breather.

"Shots! Shots! Shots!" She yelled as she snapped her fingers and danced toward me. The music was loud so I couldn't hear what she was saying. I just read her lips. When she made it to the table, she grabbed my hand and pulled me to the bar with her. After downing three shots of Effen Vodka, I let Candace talk me into approaching Corey.

"Just go talk to him. Stop waiting on these niggas. Its 2016, girl. Women are aggressive these days. You have to go after what you want."

"But what if he disses me?" I asked.

"But what if he doesn't?" She retorted.

So I did it. I took a chance and went over to say hello. A simple hello turned into an hour long conversation. He told me he had a girlfriend. I told him I had a man. Yet, somehow when he asked me to leave the club with him, I did. In that moment Shawn didn't matter. Corey's girlfriend, Felicia didn't matter. I knew I looked like a whore that night, but I took it to another level and acted like one when I left with him. I couldn't help it though; nothing in me was able to tell Corey no.

On the ride my mind raced. I didn't know this man. He was a stranger and I was alone in the car with him, on the way to a hotel. Was I safe? I'd never had a one night stand before but I knew that's where this was headed. What about Shawn? What would I tell him the next morning? Wait… what if Corey sexed me and left as soon as it was over? Could I handle that? I wasn't sure about anything other than I wanted every minute I could get with him. So if this is what it took, then I would do it and worry about the consequences later.

"Damn, girl. Why you gotta feel so good," Corey panted as he moved slowly inside of me. I was on cloud nine and climbing higher with every stroke of his pelvis. I gyrated my hips, matching him stroke for stroke. That made him move harder and faster until we both came. He pressed his body into mine and nibbled softly on my left ear before planting a trail of kisses from my twin peaks to my belly button. He moved about my body as if we'd known each other for years, making me tingle all over.

"I can't take much more," I whispered as he leaned into me.

He laughed half-heartedly and rolled off me. I expected him to sit up on the side of the bed, slide into his pants, and hit me with some lame excuse about why he couldn't stay. But he didn't. After we washed up and he'd flushed the condom, he got back in bed and we cuddled until we both passed out cold.

Six Months Later…

Relief washed over me when I heard the front door slam. I turned back around to check my reflection in the mirror one last time. I pressed my lips together to be sure my lip gloss was right. The door slamming meant Shawn had just left. I rushed to the bedroom to grab my purse because I was leaving right behind him. Then I heard keys jingling in the door. That meant Shawn was back.

"Ughhh," I said aloud when the door opened. "He makes me so sick," I continued, talking to myself but secretly hoping Shawn heard me and took the hint.

I wished like hell every day that he would just leave me alone. But he wouldn't go away. I had spent many days cooped up alone in this very condo waiting for my man to walk through that door. I spent way too many nights waiting to confront his ass as soon as that door opened. Now the opposite was true. I couldn't get rid of him no matter how hard I tried. We'd already spent the majority of the day fussing about everything and nothing. So when dusk fell and I was in the bedroom picking out my club attire for the night, it was war!

"I don't know why you're digging around in that closet. Yo' ass ain't going out tonight!" Shawn yelled, making his way into our walk in closet.

I laughed because he sounded so stupid. I'd already picked my dress and it was lying neatly across the bed. I was in my closet looking for the perfect shoes to accentuate the red pin stripes in my dress. I grabbed a pair of leather, peep-toe sling backs and walked back toward the front of the closet where Shawn was blocking the door.

"You ain't going nowhere so you might as well put those shoes back on the rack," he said, trying to take them from me. "And when did you start wearing heels anyway? You think you slick! Don't make me beat yo' ass."

"Don't make me call Jerome!"

I knew that would piss him off. My brother, Jerome had put his hands on Shawn a few years back. It was a sore topic for Shawn and it was the first thing I said every time he made me mad.

"Call yo' brother. That nigga ain't shit."

I laughed again because me and Shawn both knew he didn't mean that.

"Okay," I said sarcastically, making my way out of the closet past him. Lucky for him, I didn't feel like ruining the night or I would have called my brother. I grabbed a very sexy, lace bra and panty set from the drawer, then as I turned to get my dress, I caught a glimpse of Shawn sitting on the edge of the bed looking pitiful. That's when I noticed he was kind of funny-looking. Something about his head shape was off. His ears were big. And he was skinny. I was grossed out and couldn't believe I'd ever been attracted to Shawn.

"Oh my gosh, Shawn. Please just leave. Where are your boys? Can't you find someone to go play pool or something? It's funny how you used to always have somewhere to go and something to do. You never had time for me. Why don't you get dressed and go to the strip club or something? Go make it rain on them hoes! Ain't that what you used to do? Or better yet, you can stay here while I go out. Get a taste of your own medicine and spend some lonely nights. I don't really care what you do, but I'm going out. Cased closed!"

Shawn didn't say a word. He got up, grabbed the keys to his Impala, and slammed the door behind him. That made me happy!

When the keys jingled and Shawn walked back through the door, I was disgusted. But it really didn't matter what he did. I was going out regardless because I had a date with Corey and nothing was going to stop that.

Corey and I had been inseparable since the night we met and had been sneaking around for months. We stayed nights at hotels, had lunch together, and went to the movies with no remorse. When we were together we behaved as if we were a couple, unbothered by the fact that we were cheating with each other.

It took six months for Shawn to notice. Six whole months for him to realize that I wasn't just sitting in the house waiting on his punk ass anymore. It only hit him that something was awry because he'd planned a romantic dinner for the two of us and this time he showed up but I didn't.

Just think, the morning after I was with Corey for the first time, I cried the entire ride home. He called me an Uber because there was no way I was going to let him drop me off at home. For one, I didn't want him to know where I lived just yet and for two, I didn't want Shawn to see a dude bringing me home after being out all night. I was so worried about facing Shawn that I'd concocted this entire story about how I'd drank so much that I passed out at Candace's crib. I could feel the adrenaline wash over me as I unlocked the door to our condo. Fear made my heart speed up. But it was all for nothing because Shawn wasn't home either.

For some reason, it hurt me that Shawn wasn't there to notice I'd spent the night out. I wanted to see him upset about it because I needed to know he cared. Instead, he didn't notice for six months. By then, I'd fallen in love with Corey.

Corey

At twenty-four, I couldn't believe I was still with Felicia. We hooked up in high school when we were both seventeen. Back when I was young, dumb, and full of cum. Not that things are much different for me now, it's just I can't believe she has hung on for seven years. Felicia is beautiful. Her full breasts sit up on her chest like headlights, she has a coke bottle shape and her caramel skin pairs perfectly with her dark brown hair and eyes. Her dad is black but her mom is Asian, so her eyes have a slight slant. She is perfect mind, body and soul. She doesn't have a blemish anywhere and I love her.

I've always told myself that if Felicia could hang on until we were at least twenty-five, I'd pop the question and make her my wife. I knew she wanted to walk away plenty of days, but she never did. That's why I called her my ride or die. I didn't feel like she would ever leave me or that I would ever leave her. Those other chicks were just things to do. I never fell in love with any of them... until I met Yvette.

Something was just different about Yvette. In the looks department, she couldn't compete with Felicia. At best, Yvette was average looking. When she approached me at the club, I talked to her as a joke. My boys had been busting funnies all night because we all noticed Yvette was staring at me. My cousin, Joe-Joe bet me a stack that I wouldn't skip over Brandi, who was all over me that night too and get with Yvette instead. Not one to pass up on that dough, I took the bet.

Once I started talking to her though, I realized she was a nice person and we had a lot in common. Then things escalated when she whipped it on me that night in the hotel. I fell for her hard. Suddenly, I didn't care as much about Felicia anymore. I wanted to give Yvette all my time. So that's what I did.

Yvette

"Couldn't you get used to this?" I asked Corey as I fed him a strawberry from the fruit tray I'd made. Strawberries and whip cream were part of our dessert after a candlelit dinner. I sat across from him in my black bra and panty set. He made me feel more beautiful than I ever had so I was able to do sexy things like this. My plan was to seduce him into leaving Felicia. I'd had enough of being his side chick. I loved Corey and I knew he loved me.

"This is perfect, baby. I could be with you forever," he answered, leaning in to kiss me. His lips were sweet from remnants of strawberry juice.

"So what's stopping you?" I asked full well knowing the answer. Over the past few months, things for me and Corey had moved pretty fast. This was a conversation we'd had several times and every time it didn't end well.

"Really Yvette? Do we have to do this again? I've told you over and over that I love you and I want to be with you one day, but I can't just leave Felicia after seven years together. She deserves more from me than for me to leave her now." Corey's voice was full of hostility as he lit the blunt he'd rolled before we started dinner.

I reached up and took the blunt from him. I hit it one time before he took it back.

"Girl, give me my shit. You know you don't smoke and I'm not about to have you wasting my loud."

He laughed a little when he said it but I knew he was serious, so I did as I was told and gave it back.

"It's just that you're stressing me out. I figured a little weed might calm my nerves."

"I'm stressing you out? I just don't understand how you could sit here and say that with a straight face. You're asking me to just wake up one day and leave a seven-year relationship, but somehow I'm stressing you out. Boy, I tell you Yvette. Sometimes, I wish…"

I stood up. Corey was on my last damn nerve acting like I had nothing to lose in this. "Okay Corey. You act like I'm not going to break it off with someone. Do I have to remind you that I have a boyfriend? I'm willing to leave him today, if necessary. You're not the only one leaving someone behind."

Corey pulled himself up from the floor and stood directly in front of me with a finger to the face. "I know you're not comparing our situations. You want me to up and leave a woman who has been with me through thick and thin for the past seven years. Just up and walk out on her. And you're comparing that to you and punk ass Shawn's two-year fiasco. Obviously shit ain't all gravy with that nigga or you wouldn't be here with me. It's no comparison. So stop."

"Do you love me, Corey?" I couldn't think of anything else to say that could possibly diffuse the situation. Corey always got so defensive when it came to Felicia. It made me jealous to no end.

"I gotta go," Corey said. He turned away from me, picked up his white t-shirt and threw it over his head.

"So you're leaving? What about the rest of the night? I put all of this together and spent money on this room just for us to spend a couple of hours, is that what you're telling me?" I walked toward him. I didn't want him to leave so I leaned in for a hug.

He pulled me in and squeezed me tight. That's the one thing I loved most about Corey. He was affectionate and he didn't like to see me sad. He kissed me on the forehead before he spoke again.

"Listen Yvette. I love the hell out of you, but don't forget you came into this knowing that I had a girlfriend. I didn't lie to you at all. I didn't tell you things were bad. I didn't say I wanted to leave her. This started out as a one-night stand, but you won my heart. Let's just dead this conversation about me leaving Felicia and take this thing one day at a time. If it's too much for you, then maybe we should cut ties at this point."

Corey

I walked out on Yvette once I told her we should cut ties. I have to admit, I had fallen for her hard and fast, but leaving Felicia and making Yvette my main chick wasn't on my top list of priorities. I was still trying to get used to the fact that I started liking her ass for real, anyway. The bet with Joe-Joe had gone way too far. Matter of fact, none of my boys knew I was still dealing with Yvette. Since me and Yvette were both involved with other people, keeping our relationship on the low was a mutual idea, so I didn't have to make excuses to her for why I wouldn't take her around my family and friends. Sure I took her out, but Houston was a big city and all my peeps lived on the South side. Me and Yvette always kicked it on the North. Chances were slim that anybody I fooled with would see us. And if they did, nobody would ever suspect I would get with Yvette. She wasn't my type. I messed with bad chicks. The hard to get chicks. Beautiful, sexy, and smart. Lady in the street, freak in the sheets. Yvette is… well, she is ugly. This shit had been happening for six months too long and I wanted to find a way out without breaking her heart. I liked her but things were moving too fast.

I kind of felt bad when I left her at the hotel crying. I mean, I spent many nights of pillow talk listening to how Shawn had ruined her self-esteem. I hated that nigga for that and I always said if the opportunity presented itself, I was going to whoop his ass. Now here I was, making her feel the exact same way.

My pocket vibrated, pulling me away from my thoughts of Yvette.

I reached in and grabbed my phone. I answered without looking at the screen. I already knew it was Brandi.

"What up?" I said, throwing the phone up to my ear.

I was right. It was Brandi. I knew it was her because she'd been blowing me up for about three hours. I knew she was going to be pissed and I didn't feel like hearing all that cussing about how I had hurt her. Brandi should have been tired of me by now. She was another chick I was hitting that wanted to be my woman. She came into this knowing I had a girlfriend, but just like the rest she was cool with it for about three months, then she fell in love with a nigga and thought she was going to be the one to make me leave Felicia. And just like the rest, she was disappointed. I had no intention of ever leaving my main chick.

"Again, Corey? For real? You just gonna do this to me again? You just gonna tell me you're coming and not show up. You said you would be here by 8:30. You said you wouldn't stand me up tonight. You said you wasn't going let me down. But here it is midnight and yo' ass still ain't here. It's fucking midnight Corey, and you are just now even answering the phone. I've been calling and texting since 9:00. You didn't even..."

I hung up the phone before she could finish the last sentence. I already knew what she was going to say. "You didn't have the decency to just let me know you were ok. I was worried about you Corey," I said aloud in my best "Brandi" impersonation. She said the same shit every time. Once she got that out, then the tears came. And I didn't feel like none of that shit tonight. I wanted some drinks and a good time, so I called Gina.

Gina

I was in bed when my phone rang. I was drained, but I answered the phone anyway simply because it was Corey. I always answered when Corey called. Everybody did. That's the very same reason why I opened the door thirty minutes later, too. Because it was Corey.

He was my sanity. The dude who never let me down because he was the dude I never expected anything from. No expectations meant no let downs.

Corey kissed me on the cheek and walked right past me into the kitchen as soon as I opened the door.

"Well, make yourself at home why don't you?" I said, giving him a fake smile.

"I am at home; so why wouldn't I get comfortable?" He asked popping the top on a Bud Light.

"Paying a little rent here and there doesn't make you my roommate Corey. Paying rent just allows you to visit."

Corey grabbed the remote, kicked his feet out of his Jordan's and up onto my coffee table.

"What you been up to tonight?" Corey asked, totally disregarding my comments.

"I was in bed."

"In bed?"

"Yes. In bed, I'm exhausted," I whined. Then I plopped down in his lap.

Corey pulled me close and planted kisses all over my face. I giggled and begged him to stop even though I didn't really want him to. Corey tickled me a little as he kissed me and I giggled harder.

After he tickled his way into my panties, I got up, fixed him a sandwich, rolled a blunt, and brought him a beer like I always did. Once he was full, he got up, threw on his pants, and left me in the middle of the night.... Like he always did.

Yvette

I didn't talk to Corey for two months after he walked out on me. If he wanted to cut ties, then that's what we would do. At least that's what I told myself at first. *I hated him. I was never talking to him again. I didn't need him. He was selfish.* I filled my head with things to help me move on. I didn't call or text. I stayed busy. I tried to focus on Shawn.

*****

Shawn and I walked hand in hand into Pappadeaux's, which happened to be my favorite little seafood place. Yes, I was being nicer to Shawn. We talked and decided we would work harder on our relationship. I really didn't want to be with him anymore, but he was the best option I had for getting over Corey. So I had to do what I had to do.

The first thing I did was order a drink. I needed it after the day I was having. As the waitress took us to our table, I spotted Corey skinning and grinning with some chick. And it wasn't Felicia. Now that… That hurt me to the core. I mean, I knew I was Corey's number 2 behind Felicia and I was cool with that. But I never, ever expected to be number 3, 4, or 5. I thought Felicia was my only competition. Turns out I was very wrong.

I tried to enjoy dinner with Shawn, but there was no way that was happening with Corey in the same restaurant so I told Shawn I didn't feel well and I wanted to go home. To my surprise, he didn't complain.

I almost felt guilty for lying to Shawn about being sick, but I convinced myself that it wasn't really a lie, since technically I WAS sick. I mean, I did throw up a little in my mouth twice at the thought of Corey and some skanky side piece.

Corey

That was it. I was caught red-handed. I just knew shit was about to hit the fan when I looked up and saw Yvette walking into Pappadeaux's with Shawn. I knew who that nigga was, but he had no clue about me. It pissed me off to see Yvette gallivanting around town with that punk, but I kept my cool. After all, I couldn't really spaz out like I wanted to with Brandi sitting across the table from me. This trip to Pappadeaux's was a makeup date because I stood her up the last time. She was too easy. Date night to a seafood restaurant was all it took for me to make my way back into Brandi's bed.

When I saw Yvette, I prepared myself for a confrontation. I had my lie all mapped out. But nothing happened. There was absolutely no yelling, or fussing, or cussing. Nothing. Not long after Yvette and that nigga walked into the restaurant, they left.

Just as my nerves settled, Brandi spoke up.

"Here comes ya girl." She nodded her head toward the door that Yvette had just walked out of.

My heart dropped. I couldn't believe Yvette would react in front of Shawn. I stood defensively to face her head on. Instead of Yvette, I saw Donna.

Donna was Brandi's older sister. I banged her once when I was fourteen; before I really even knew what to do. When I first hooked up with Brandi they fought twice. Now they don't speak. I didn't understand it at all. I had to remind Donna a few times that we were kids when everything went down. It had all happened more than ten years ago, but she said Brandi was foul anyway. She said sisters shouldn't go behind each other no matter when it was. I didn't give a damn either way. Neither of them would ever be my woman, so in my opinion there was nothing to fight about.

To my surprise, there was no drama. Donna walked past us and smirked. Brandi called her a bitch under her breath, but nothing popped off.

Yvette

I was sick for a week after I saw Corey at the restaurant. It hit me when I got home that the chick he was with was the same girl who was dancing all over him at the club. It literally hurt me so bad that I lay in bed for five or six days with the lights out, the blinds closed, and the TV playing on mute. The only time I moved was to check my phone for messages from Corey. Shawn took care of me like I had the flu. Poor idiot.

This morning, I woke up with a new attitude. There was no way on the planet I would let a man make me sick. Why was I lying in bed, whining and crying over a man that ain't crying over me? Even worse, he's not my man. He's Felicia's man. So these tears should be hers. Not mine.

I looked over at Shawn's peanut head and big ears as he slept beside me. I thought about all the stuff I'd been through with him and decided I didn't want to work things out. He wasn't worth all I had been through. I deserved better. My mind raced. I didn't care that he was trying now. It was too late. Where had he been all those lonely nights? Where had he been our whole relationship?

I wanted out of this thing with Shawn. I wanted Corey. And I was going to do whatever I had to do to get him.

Corey

I pulled up to the house just in time to catch Felicia dumping the last of my things all over the balcony. Shoes, clothes, jewelry, and underwear decorated the yard. It was a *Love and Hip Hop Atlanta* moment. Remember that scene with Joc and Khadiyah? Yea. That was us.

I didn't want to go in the house. I didn't want to see the tears fall or hear her voice crack. I didn't want to witness the pain caused by me. I didn't know what had set her off. I wondered what she had seen or heard. Tried figuring out where I had slipped up before I stuck my key in the door knob, headed to face her.

I didn't have to wonder long because the moment I opened the door she was right there waiting.

"Who the hell is this bitch?" She asked, shoving her iPhone so close to my face that I couldn't make out what she was showing me.

"Hold up!" I said, slightly annoyed. I took the phone from her hand to take a better look.

Facebook. Damn! Facebook. And Brandi. I had been so careful. I told all of my side pieces that I didn't do social media. Told them over and over that I didn't want pictures of me on Facebook, Instagram, Snapchat. Nowhere. And it had worked until now. There was nothing I could say that would make sense. It was right there plain as day. I was hugged up with Brandi at Relentless, a club we went to when we took a quick trip to the Dallas area. I was on business and Brandi was arm candy.

"Ummm." I couldn't think of anything. I stroked my chin, hoping it would stimulate my brain so I could open my mouth and talk my way out of this. But nothing happened.

"Ummm, what? Ummm, what Corey? Can't talk? Cat got your tongue? Well, you don't have to. I'm so over this shit Corey that there is nothing left to say. I'm not arguing with you. I don't care anymore. I want you to get your things and leave. We're done."

Deep in my heart of hearts, I knew Felicia didn't mean any of this. She was just angry. And deep down inside she wanted me to beg her for forgiveness just as I had done all those times before. But this time, I didn't do any of that. Felicia was a good girl. She deserved better. And although I had no intention of ever leaving her for another woman, that didn't mean I wouldn't go if she kicked me out. So I left.

I called Yvette and asked if she could meet up. I needed to see her. I wanted to apologize to her for the way I'd been acting. Then I called Brandi and got deep in her shit for sharing pictures of me on social media. She tried to deny posting pictures of me, but I didn't let her finish. I told her I would kick her ass if she didn't take every last picture of me off the internet, and then I hung up in her face. It wasn't worth my time to listen to her lie.

Yvette

Everything was working just as I had planned. I had asked around about Brandi and found out my cousin Jasmine actually knew her…

And they were friends on Facebook. I asked Jasmine if I could log onto her page and snoop on Brandi. You know the old saying, if you go looking, you will find? Well, I found a picture of Corey's cheating ass hugged all up on Brandi at some nightclub. It pissed me off to no end.

I don't take pictures. I don't do Facebook; that shit is for women. Men don't put their business all over the internet. Those were all of the excuses Corey had made to me when I tried to get pics of us. I was fuming, because here he was, right in my face, smiling at the camera while someone got a snapshot of him and Brandi.

My fingers moved on their own. I created a fake email address so I could create a fake "Brandi" Facebook page. I cropped the picture of Brandi and Corey and made it the cover photo. I stole about a hundred of Brandi's photos, added some friends, spent about two weeks making statuses that would make the page look legitimate, and then I sent Felicia a friend request. After all that, I waited for shit to hit the fan and Corey to run right into my arms.

Only two days after I sent the friend request Corey was blowing up my phone. I let him call multiple times before I answered. I didn't want that nigga thinking I needed him (even though I felt like I did). When I finally picked up, he gave me this whole song and dance about how he loved me and he missed me. He apologized that I saw him at Pappadeaux's with that Brandi chick, but never once mentioned anything about he and Felicia breaking up. Then he asked to meet up. And I agreed.

Brandi

"It seems like things are going from bad to worse," I mumbled to myself as I leaned against the granite-topped counter in my bathroom. First, Corey called screaming on me about a picture I posted of us months ago. I knew I wasn't supposed to have it on Facebook but I thought I'd marked it private so only my friends could see and I wasn't friends with him or anybody he socialized with on Facebook. Hell, I knew the rules of being a side chick meant I couldn't post or show public displays of affection with him. But somehow, some way, the picture had been leaked and Corey was pissed. But little did he know those social media pictures were the least of our worries.

I moved over to the toilet, pulled my pants down and took a seat. I was glad I'd decided to buy the box that contained two pregnancy tests. I had to have confirmation that I was really carrying his baby before I told Corey. I grabbed the disposable cup and pissed inside. There was no way on planet earth, I was going to try to hold that little plastic stick in place long enough and still enough to hit the tip, so I pee'd in a cup and dipped the stick. I put the cap on, sat it on the counter and walked out. No sooner than I plopped down on my bed, I got up again and anxiously walked back to the bathroom. It didn't take as long as the directions stated because the moment I looked down, the digital screen displayed the word: PREGNANT.

The room rocked. Time stood still. I didn't know how or if I would tell Corey. I knew with every ounce of my being that he loved

Felicia and even a baby wouldn't make him leave her, but I also knew that Corey loved kids and I had to give him the opportunity to decide if he wanted to be a part of this baby's life. I loved him too much not to tell him, but I had to wait for the right time and that wasn't now.

I needed to think. I had to come up with a plan and usually a glass of wine and a blunt helped me through difficult times. But since I couldn't have those things, I opted for a shower.

The warm water pellets beat down on my head and gently slid down my neck, chest, back, and butt. I took it in bead for bead as I used my sponge to lather soap all over me, rinse it off and lather again. I was doing everything I could to become one with the shower. It was my hope that I could melt into it and twirl down the drain into nowhere. At this point anything was better than the reality I was about to face.

Yvette

I bobbed my head and rapped with Drake as I drove along the freeway headed to meet Corey. I can't lie, he killed Meek Mill with his new cut Back to Back. By the time Drake had finished with Meek I felt kind of sorry for him but that didn't make me stop listening to this song on repeat. I exited the freeway for the feeder road and checked my reflection in the rearview mirror when I got to the stoplight. I wasn't one for wearing makeup, but today was a special day so I'd applied a little eyeliner, mascara, and lip gloss. My reflection showed that my lip gloss was poppin' so I was good.

As I pulled up to the mall, I swallowed back the guilt I felt about creating that fake "Brandi" page. I knew it was wrong, but I had to pat myself on the back for doing what it took to win my man. That page killed two birds with one stone. I knew Corey would dump Brandi for posting on Facebook and I hoped Felicia would spaz on Corey when she saw it. If my plan worked, Brandi and Felicia would both be gone and I would have my man to myself.

When Corey called and asked me to meet up he tried me with that going out to a restaurant shit. I laughed a little before I responded. Just who the hell did Corey take me for? I wasn't Brandi, you don't make up to me with a seafood platter. Making up to me meant a shopping spree, so I told him to come to the Galleria.

"Damn, I miss that nigga," I said as I took one last glance in my rearview mirror before I got out of the car. That was the honest to

God truth. It was crazy because I'd spent all that time with Shawn and when I put him out the house, I didn't miss him for one day. But then along came Corey and when he wasn't around, I missed everything about him. I missed his voice, his smile, his touch, his love. I missed everything. And that's why I did what I did to get him back.

I asked Corey to meet me at the Chanel store. Like I said before, I'm not an extravagant fashion chick, but I wanted Corey to pay for the pain I'd suffered after seeing him with Brandi. There was a small $3,000 quilted leather Caviar bag that I wanted him to buy. That was the way I wanted him to prove his love.

Corey walked in with his jeans sagging, no belt, an oversized Polo, and a pair of white Air Force Ones. Of course he adorned the flashy piece and chain. His attire for the day was somewhat of a turn off. I hated that he was looking like the stereotypical hood nigga from early 2000, but I rushed up to him anyway. I needed to hug him. I needed him to pull me close and hold me so I could smell the scent of his cologne. The feel of his skin against mine made me want to cry. Tears threatened to fill my eyes, but I blinked them away as I tried to step back from Corey. He didn't let me go. He wrapped his arms tightly around my body, so I lay my head gently on his strong chest and didn't move a muscle until he spoke.

"I missed you baby," Corey said softly as he looked in my eyes and pecked my lips.

"Missed you too," I answered.

"Grab what you want real quick and let's get out of here, I have another surprise for you."

I wasn't too happy about the "grab what you want real quick" comment. Grabbing something fast wasn't my idea of a shopping spree, but the fact that Corey said he had another surprise is what helped me keep my composure. Besides, I already knew what I wanted so I had the clerk to ring up the purse. Corey paid her then I followed him through the mall to the...

Food court?

Did Corey really just pull me out of the Chanel store to give me a gift in the freaking food court?

With a frown on my face, I dipped a few waffle fries from Chick-fil-A into some ketchup. I was beyond pissed. I told Corey I wasn't meeting at no restaurant for make-up dinner and he brought me to a freaking fast food restaurant in the mall. I stared at him long and hard. If looks could kill Corey would have died instantly.

Then without speaking, he stood from his seat and pulled a little black jewelry box from his pocket...

Corey

Even though Yvette did everything she could to avoid having a makeup dinner, she and I ended up having lunch in the food court at the Galleria mall. When she asked me to meet her at the Chanel store, I knew I was going to have to come off a wad, but it didn't matter. I loved Yvette and I knew I had some making up to do.

She was pissed about the Chick-Fil-A. Her eyes pierced my soul. I was scared low-key. I had just dropped three stacks on a purse no bigger than the size of a mass market paperback book and she had the nerve to be upset about eating at Chick-Fil-A. I wanted to go off, but I knew when I handed her the black box, things would be ok so I refrained. Her angry glare turned to a half-smile. It was obvious she was confused. I'm sure she thought the box contained jewelry of some sort, but it didn't. Inside was something much better. It was the key to my new apartment. Our apartment. I had rented a spacious luxury apartment fifteen stories up with a view over Buffalo Bayou. The Sovereign at Regent Square is one of Houston's best. It's a modern high rise with all the trimmings: large floor to ceiling windows with nice views of the Houston skyline, an illuminated seventy-five feet lap pool surrounded by palm trees and gorgeous pool furniture, a community fire pit, and a twenty-four-hour fitness center open only to residents. Felicia had begged for a place there. It was her dream. I loved Felicia, yet somehow I found myself offering this to Yvette.

"What is this, Corey?" She asked, slightly baffled.

"It's a key."

"A key? A key. I don't know what to say. What does this mean, baby?"

"It means you get what you want. I'm done with Felicia. It's just me and you now. I got us a luxury apartment at The Sovereign."

She smiled real big. I had made her happy. I just hoped I was making the right decision for the both of us.

Yvette

Corey made a boss move when he gave me a key to one of the nicest apartments in Houston. I was hesitant to take it at first. I mean, Corey still hadn't mentioned what happened with him and Felicia. Although I was pretty sure they broke up about the post of him and Brandi on Facebook, I wanted confirmation. In a sick sort of way, I hoped that wasn't really it. I wanted him to leave Felicia because that's what he wanted to do, not because I had forced his hand.

"You ok baby?" Corey asked.

"Yea. I'm good."

"Then why are you so quiet? I thought you would be happy. I got us a place. I gave you a key and you're just sitting there silently."

"I'm sorry baby. I'm just so happy. I don't know what to say." I leaned in to kiss him, but he cautiously pulled back. "Oh shit!" Corey exclaimed.

I looked behind me and Felicia was walking into the food court. I tried to act like I wasn't tripping, but deep down I was super nervous. I took a sip of my lemonade and dipped another waffle fry in my ketchup. Corey looked uncomfortable, but he didn't say anything else. I know he wanted to get up and run away from the table, but he sat dumbfounded. I'm guessing he was hoping she didn't spot us.

But she did…

I jumped to my feet, knocking my lemonade off the table. I wasn't about to give that bitch a chance to sneak me. Corey didn't move.

"Really, Corey?" She asked the moment she stepped up.

Corey's punk ass didn't speak. He stood there with eyes the size of saucers, looking like someone had knocked the wind out of him.

"Is this what you've been up to? Please tell me you haven't been seeing this bald headed troll. Seeing you here with her is so insulting. At least the Facebook THOT was pretty. This bitch looks like Grace Jones."

I laughed. Not because it was funny, but because it was easier to laugh than to cry. I had been called ugly all my life and I was tired of it. I had to defend myself, so I decided to get her where it would hurt and fighting wasn't the answer.

"Well, Cinderella. This bald headed troll just took your man!" I reached over to the table and picked up the key. It was still in the little black box. "Corey, just gave me this key to OUR new apartment."

Felicia drew her arm back and hit me square in the nose. Blood squirted everywhere. That pissed me off. I swung back. Three quick punches about her pretty little face sent her falling back. When she fell, I started kicking her anywhere that I could. A small crowd started to gather until an older white gentleman decided to break up the fight.

Corey never moved. He stood there like an idiot and let us fight it out. In my opinion, he was a coward for that. Thank God that someone else had the decency to put an end to the madness. I picked up the key that was now on the floor and pretended to fling it through the food court.

"Fuck you Corey! It's over!" I said, before I stormed out of the mall carrying that $3000 purse. Once I was far enough away, I stuff the key inside and bolted to my car.

Corey

The day after Yvette and Felicia had that knockdown, drag out at the mall my cell phone rang nonstop. Yvette. Felicia. Brandi. Gina. Brandi. Brandi. Brandi. Brandi. Yvette. Felicia. Brandi.

I didn't answer. I couldn't face Yvette or Felicia. I wasn't in the mood for Gina. And Brandi was the cause of all this drama so I definitely didn't have time for her. After the calls, came the text messages. I didn't read them either.

I felt bad that I had let the situation between Felicia and Yvette escalate to a fight. I loved both of them and I never wanted to hurt them. I didn't know what to say or how I could face either of them, so I planned to spend a few days at a hotel until things calmed down and I could devise a plan.

My phone buzzed again. This time it was my cousin, Joe-Joe.

"What's up man?" I said into the phone.

"What's up fam? We got issues."

"Issues? What you mean?"

"Big issues. That work we got from Mannie ain't cooking up right. As it stands right now, we looking at losing about fifty bands. That nigga ain't answering none of my calls, which makes me feel like he knew this shit wasn't right. I'm on the verge of running up in that nigga spot on some Shotta's type shit, but I wanted to holla at you first."

Joe-Joe talked hard and fast so I knew it was serious. But I wasn't one to bring drama that could hurt my business. I didn't want Joe-Joe to do anything that could bring the heat and shut down our operation. Joe-Joe is a real goon, that nigga wouldn't think twice about running up in Mannie's strip joint and killing everybody in that thang. I was a more calculated playa. I wanted to hit that nigga and get away with it, so I told Joe-Joe to hold off. I needed some time to put something together and I would get back with him on our next move. Joe-Joe agreed and we disconnected.

Brandi

"Can I get some space? You're making me nervous," I said to Corey as he stood over me while I sat on the toilet.

"Girl. Just pee in the cup," he demanded. "If you ain't lying to a nigga, it ain't nothing to be nervous about."

I had been calling Corey over and over since the moment I found out I was pregnant. Every time he hit the reject button, I would hang up and redial. I needed to talk to him about this baby. He deserved to know we were going to be parents and I deserved to know how he would feel about it so I kept calling. He never answered, but he popped up at my apartment not long ago trying to hug on me so I took that opportunity to drop the bomb on him.

Of course he didn't believe me. But I told him I was 100% sure and showed him both of the tests that I had already taken.

"Pregnant, Corey. Both of these tests confirm I'm having your baby."

I could see the angst fill his eyes. Corey didn't want a baby. The look on his face made that abundantly clear. He left my place in a fury and came back in an even worse mood with a plastic Wal-Green's bag full of pregnancy tests of all different brands clenched between his fingers.

I didn't understand why he was standing over me while I pee'd on this test. We had been at this for hours. There were three positive tests sitting on the bathroom counter. One showed the word: PREGNANT. The other had a plus sign. Another was two pink lines. But no matter how we sliced it, they all meant I was knocked up and Corey was the father.

"I'm not nervous about the results Corey. I'm nervous because you're standing over me with your hands balled into fists, forcing me to take a fourth test. Nothing's gonna change. I'm pregnant, baby. It is what it is."

I said that to Corey hoping to calm him down some. Then I did as I was told and wet the tip of the last pregnancy test with my pee.

When the word "yes" showed up on the screen, Corey got even more upset.

"Ok. So you're pregnant. How do I know it's mine? Bitches are known for trying to trap a nigga with a baby. I can't tell you how many of the homies claimed babies that didn't belong to them and they didn't find out until it was too late."

"The baby is yours, Corey."

"Yea. We'll see about that!" Corey shook his head, walked out of the bathroom, grabbed his car keys and cell phone then headed toward the front door. After he opened the door and walked out, he turned around and said, "I don't trust no drug store pregnancy test. Make a doctor's appointment and let me know when it is."

Before I could respond, he closed the door in my face.

I was relieved when he left. I even smiled a little. Corey's reaction wasn't as bad as I expected. In fact, it was better. Him asking me to make a doctor's appointment gave me more hope than if he'd told me to get an abortion like I thought he would. Maybe this thing with me and Corey would pan out. Maybe a baby would bring us together and get rid of Felicia. Only time would tell.

Corey

Damn! A baby? If it wasn't one thing it was another. When I left the hotel headed to Brandi's crib, my intention was to hug and kiss on her a little and soften her up because I needed her help to carry out this hit on Mannie. Most of the time a beautiful woman is any man's Kryptonite and Brandi was gorgeous. I needed her to infiltrate Mannie's operation and get me the information I needed to take him down. But I get there and the bitch started talking all this crazy stuff about a fucking baby. And that was the last thing I needed.

I drove back to the hotel to think. The whole way, I played that old hit, *Confessions* by Usher, on repeat. It summed up my situation in a nutshell. If Brandi was really pregnant that could mess up a lot of stuff. I didn't need that in my life right now. It would kill Felicia. And Yvette. They would both hate me and probably never speak to me again and I would be stuck taking care of a baby with Brandi's thotting and bopping ass.

But then again, I can't say it would be a bad thing to have my own little nigga. I smiled a tad at the thought of having my own flesh and blood to carry on my name. I didn't want to slang yay for the rest of my life. I needed to launder some of this dope money into a legitimate business. I wanted something low-key but that would bring in a lot of money. I had thought about investing in a few of those automatic car washes or a janitorial service since car washes are seasonal. Joe-Joe always cracked on me when I talked about it, but I had dreams of doing more than this drug game shit and a baby would give me an even bigger reason to get out.

The game provided more than enough money for me to take care of my seed. But the way things were going in these streets, chances were slim that I would be here to raise him and there was no way on God's green earth that I was gonna leave my lil man in this cruel world to fend for himself.

That's it. I had no choice but to move in on Mannie and take him out. I had nine months to get my shit together and the fastest way would be to dead Mannie. I had every reason to. For one, he put me on some waste that could kill my business and for two, I had to straighten up to take care of my seed. I hated to do it, but after Brandi's appointment, I was going to convince her to go at Mannie for me. I knew it would be dangerous, but it was our only way out.

Yvette

Ever since the other day when I was forced to knock Felicia's ass out in the middle of the mall, I had been feeling the lowest of the low. All I could do was sit in the house and stare at that key, thinking about all that had gone on. I wondered if I had done something wrong. I couldn't convince myself that Felicia deserved to see me with Corey in that way. Or that she and I should have fought.

I knew she was still hurting over the incident with seeing Brandi affectionately locked arm in arm with a man that had been hers for over seven years. And I knew I was the only reason she was ever exposed to that pain. In her mind, I was just another slut that Corey was hooking up with. She didn't know that he loved me and that I loved him. She didn't know this was a situation where Corey and I had a full-fledged six-month relationship. In her mind, I was probably meeting him in nasty roach-infested motels for quick rolls in the hay. She was clueless.

Or was I?

I knew Corey had a reputation for being a ladies' man, but I allowed myself to get caught up in love with him. I allowed him to make me feel like I was special. I was in love with the idea of a man like Corey being mine. I wondered how many women there were. Then decided that I didn't really want to know. I shook my head to lose the thoughts.

I picked up my cell to call Corey for the hundredth time. He didn't answer. I knew he was avoiding me and it hurt like hell. I thought about calling my brother and telling a lie so he would bust Corey up, but figured I wouldn't because I still loved him and I wasn't ready to lose him just yet. I sat the phone back down on the dining room table and walked toward my bar to pour a drink. Before I could get too far gone, my phone started to ring and I lunged toward it hoping it was Corey. When I got a glance at the caller ID, I noticed it was Shawn and rejected the call.

My phone chirped indicating I had a voice message. Holding a glass of vodka on the rocks, I listened to Shawn's message.

"Yvette. I know you're avoiding me. I just want to tell you that I love you girl. And I miss you… I wish you would pick up the phone. All a brother needs is one more chance to make this right. Come on boo. Call me back. I need you and…"

I deleted the message before he could finish. Shawn had his chance. I wasn't living in the past anymore it was time to move forward. He didn't appreciate me when he had me and I was done.

When I finished the first glass of vodka, I said forget it and started drinking from the bottle. Alone and confused, I drank and drank until I passed out cold.

I woke up the next morning with a pounding headache and an upset stomach, but still yet, I was a bitch on a mission. I threw up, downed some Alka-Seltzer, took a shower, and ran a pick through my mini fro. Then I pulled out a plain cotton tee with the words:

#BLACKLIVESMATTER printed across the front, and slid into a pair of Apple Bottom Jeans before heading for the door. By the way, of course I know people don't rock Apple Bottom Jeans anymore. That's just my style, I do exactly what I want to do when I want to do it and I don't care who cares.

I drove until I finally ended up parked on the street in front of the place where Corey had rented us an apartment. I got outside of the car and stared. Walked toward the apartment and stopped at the pool to take in the beautiful atmosphere. A lone tear made its way down my cheek. I didn't know what to do or how to react. All I knew is that I wanted to live in a place like this. No! I deserved to live in a place like this. But I had to ask myself what it would cost me to have it. I wipe my eyes before any more tears could fall. I was amazed at how bad this hurt. I loved Corey and I wanted this to work. I wanted to live in this apartment with him. Wanted to be his wife. To cook his dinner and wash his clothes. I wanted to grow old and go to Bingo. I snickered a little at the thought of me and Corey at the bingo hall.

I wanted my man even if I had to beg. Shit, desperate times call for desperate measures and I was going to win.

Corey

As soon as the door to my hotel room opened, Gina was all over me. I finally called her back after I left Brandi's place because I needed some sexual healing to take my mind off all the shit that was going on in my life. Things were in shambles with the two women I loved, Brandi was pregnant, so Gina was like a breath a fresh air. No expectations always equaled a good time.

Gina and I were naked and under the cover real quick. She was kissing and licking me in ways that I can't explain. I could barely take what she was giving so in an effort not to be a two-minute man, I took control and made my way on top of her. I trailed soft kisses from her belly button down to her thighs, lingering there just close enough to her love box to make her lose it. Gina took a deep breath, then begged me to enter her.

"I just want you to make love to me," she begged.

Make love to you? I thought to myself. That threw me for a loop. Gina had never used the words "make love". It scared me. I didn't need her falling for me, too. So much was happening around me with women wanting me to be serious with them that I couldn't stand the thought of Gina anywhere close to being like them. My attraction to her was that she was a pass and go.

I just want you to make love to me. I just want you to make love to me. I just want you to make love to me. Those words rang in my head over and over so many times that my big guy went limp. I rolled off of her and sat up on the edge of the bed. Gina crawled seductively over to me and hugged me from behind. I could feel her D cup breast against my back. Sitting up on her knees, she wrapped her arms around my neck and rubbed my chest. I have to admit, it felt good, but not good enough to forget that she had used the words "make love to me".

I didn't want to hurt her feelings but I had to find a way to get her out of my room. I covered my head with my hands and leaned forward. This was a delicate situation. I liked Gina but the timing was all wrong. The mood had changed. The thrill was gone... so I wanted her gone.

She slid out of the bed and walked around in front of me. She grabbed my hands, pulling them away from my face.

"Look at me," she said sweetly. "I'm crazy about you, Corey."

I jumped up from the bed, stunned by what she'd said. I slid my legs into my boxers and asked Gina to get dressed. Then I told her to leave. She was hesitant about leaving, and started babbling all this stuff about how we were made for each other. I'm not sure where it all came from so suddenly, but I couldn't take it. I grabbed that bitch by the arm and practically shoved her out the door. There was no more Mister Nice Guy. Gina had to go. Things had already spiraled out of control and I didn't need her adding to the confusion.

.

Brandi

Taking Corey to the doctor's office with me was absolutely the best thing that could have happened to our relationship. After Dr. Mason confirmed that I was pregnant and about six weeks along, I saw a huge change in Corey. He was so loving and attentive to me. He always answered the phone when I called and he was always willing to bring whatever I was craving, whenever I was craving it. I had more hope now than I ever did of us being a family. In fact, Corey was on his way over right now to help paint my spare bedroom.

I told him a few days ago that I'd found a neutral baby theme on Pinterest and asked if he would help me get a nursery ready. We'd agreed that we were not going to find out the gender of our bundle of joy until the day the baby entered this world. But since we had to get a room ready, I picked an aqua and grey theme that would work for a boy or a girl. I was anxious to know what I was having because I wanted a little mini me that I could dress up and treat like a princess. Of course, my baby daddy wanted a boy.

I was standing in the middle of the spare bedroom daydreaming about what life was going to be like for us when Corey walked in carrying cans of paint. I'd given him a key to my apartment because I figured we'd be living together eventually anyway. He made a trip back out to the car and came in with bags containing tarp, paint brushes, and tons of other accessories.

"Ok. Let's get this show on the road," he said and then gave me a quick peck on the cheek.

I put the tarp down over my carpet and started taping off all the areas that needed to be taped so the paint job would look clean and crisp. Once it was all set, both Corey and I started to paint. He started on the grey wall and I did the aqua.

Corey

I can't say I was excited to be having a son with Brandi. In fact, the day the doctor revealed she was actually pregnant was one of the worst days of my life. It's not that I didn't want a child. It's just that my baby mama was Brandi and not Felicia or Yvette. When I got home from finding out, I smoked three blunts back to back and downed a fifth of Henney. I thought about making her have an abortion, but I couldn't bring myself to convince a woman to rid this world of my own flesh and blood, so I told myself I needed to suck it up and be a man about it.

I still hadn't found the courage to tell Yvette or Felicia so I had been avoiding them both like the plague. Besides that, I didn't know how to face either of them after that stunt that happened at the mall.

In the meantime, I had to play along with this happy daddy façade because I still needed Brandi to help me get at that nigga Mannie. I was buttering her up a day at a time. Yesterday I popped up with all kinds of stuff for the baby. I bought a swing, a car seat, a three-month supply of diapers, a stroller, and ton of lotion, baby wash, powder and bottles. Today, I was coming through to help paint... At least that's what Brandi thought. My real reason for coming was because it was time for me to ask her to get with Mannie.

I pulled into Brandi's apartment complex and smiled. Today was the day. Joe-Joe had been blowing me up because he felt like I was moving too slow. I had pressure coming from all directions but I needed everyone to understand there was a plan and I had to follow it step by step. Mannie was going to get what was coming to him but I didn't want to fuck any of my people up in the process.

I took a deep breath as I pushed my key in the door's lock and turned the knob. I walked in to the fresh smell of recently mopped floors and Linen & Sky Scented Febreze permeating the air. I heard the familiar sounds of that song "Earned It" by the weekend. Then I saw Brandi standing in the middle of what would be our future baby's bedroom smiling and in a daze. When she turned around and saw me hauling paint, her smiled brightened and I knew immediately that today would be the day that I would make my move.

****

"That shit is crazy as hell, Corey," Brandi said as she sat up in her bed with her back against the headboard. "You gotta be kidding me."

We had finished painting the nursery and I'd put the crib together and pushed all of the furniture in place. Brandi was hungry and said she was craving Popeye's so I rushed out and got that for her. After we ate, I asked her if she would help me get to Mannie.

"All I need you to do is get as close to him as you can. Once he trusts you. I will handle the rest."

"What's the rest, baby?" Brandi asked with a look in her eyes that made me feel like she didn't want to help a brother out.

"You just let me worry about that. Are you going to help me out or nah?"

A few intense moments of silence told me that Brandi didn't want to get involved. She was scared. She'd already said that twice. But I wasn't taking no for an answer.

"I'm doing this for us, Mama." I said that, and then paused. I wanted it to soak in that I'd just called her Mama. It was obvious getting her involved was going to take a little reverse psychology. Brandi took a deep breath so I felt like I was wearing her down. That's when I decided that one thing and one thing only would go ahead and push her over the edge to my side of this discussion. I grabbed her hand and planted light kisses up her arm. Then I looked seductively into her eyes.

"This is the last piece to the puzzle, Mama. If you help me get next to Mannie, I'll be able to get out the game and be a family man. If you don't help me out, the streets win and I won't be able to be the kind of father that I need to be to my seed. My daddy wasn't shit Brandi. Last time I seen that nigga was when I was 20 and the only reason he came around then was because he heard how hard I was hitting these streets and he came through to see how much loot he could shake me for. Before that, I hadn't seen him since I was five years old. Nigga promised me a scooter and never came back. I want more than that for mine Brandi. But if you don't help me out, these streets ain't gone let me be there for him like I want to."

She smiled a little. "Who said it was gonna be a him?"

"Oh it's gonna be a junior. I'm sure of that," I said going along with her. I didn't want to push too hard. I could tell she was coming around so I changed it up a little.

Before any words could leave her lips, I pulled her up from the bed and made her face me. I tugged her shirt up over her head and my man stiffed up instantly at the sight of her boobs in a red Victoria's Secret bra. Her stomach was still flat because she was only six weeks along so she was still sexy as hell. I leaned in and bit her bottom lip just a little. Then I whispered a few sweet nothings in her ear.

"Turn around, bend over and put your hands on the bed."

Brand did exactly as commanded. I pushed her skirt up toward her waist, slid her red matching thong to the side and plunged myself deep into her. I moved gently in and out as she threw it back. I hit her from behind and massaged her breasts as I stroked. She slowly took her body all the way down to the bed and buried her face into a pillow to muffle the sounds of pleasure coming from her lips. After a few minutes, she asked me to lie down on the bed and I did. She climbed on top and looked deep into my eyes. She moved seductively and her eyes never left mine. She leaned in to kiss me and our tongues danced for what seemed like an eternity. Her eyes rolled to the back of her head.

At the height of her climax, I said, "You gone do that for me, Mama?"

"Yes! Yes! Just don't stop and I'll do whatever you want."

Just like that, my plan was in motion, and for the first time ever I spent the night at Brandi's place and held her 'til morning.

Yvette

Things were rough. Shawn had been calling me every day nonstop even though I never answered. One day when I came home from the gym, I walked up on Shawn standing in the hallway of my apartment building. I wasn't feeling that shit at all. It was almost like he was stalking me. I shook my head in disgust and tried to walk past him, but he grabbed my arm.

"What's up, Yvette? I been trying to call you." He said, looking all crazy.

"Call me for what, Shawn? I don't have time for this. Please just leave me alone. You had your chance and now it's over."

"Over? Nah. It ain't over 'til I say it's over," he said as he slid in front of my door.

"Move out of my way so I can go in the house. I'm not 'bout to stand out here and argue with you Shawn. We're done. Get over it."

No sooner than those words left my lips, Shawn had me up against the wall by the throat choking me. My legs were dangling in the air and I could barely breathe. I tried to scream but no words would escape my lips. I tugged on his hands trying to get some air. I pulled them off my neck long enough to scream at him to get off me. My heart raced. And just as I felt myself blacking out, my across the hall neighbor, Logan opened his door.

"What the hell are you doing, man? Get off of her! Let her go!"

When Shawn wouldn't release me, Logan lunged toward him and clocked him right in his left eye. Without hesitation, Shawn dropped me and returned Logan's blow, then followed it up with several more punches. Desperate to help Logan before Shawn whooped his white ass; I threw my arms around his neck and grabbed him in a chokehold. Logan's girlfriend, Molly opened the door and I yelled for her to call the police. She dialed 911 and Shawn took off.

That was enough for me. The next day I rented a U-Haul so my brother Jerome and his friends could help me move into the apartment that Corey had rented for us at The Sovereign.

Brandi

The morning after Corey tricked me into being part of his plan to take Mannie down, I got up early as hell pissed at myself about being duped. Once Corey left, I couldn't stop pacing. I walked a hole in my apartment floor from my bedroom to the living room to the kitchen. I walked and walked and walked, trying to come up with a way out of getting involved in Corey's mess.

I didn't know Mannie at all, but word on the street was that he wasn't anybody to play with. It was a known fact that he had a few bodies under his belt. Even worse, one of the people he'd killed was his very own brother for stealing from him.

The thought of me getting close to and double crossing a dude that had murked his brother made my stomach turn. I rushed to the bathroom and threw up my guts before I made it to the toilet. It could have been morning sickness but I was nearly 100% sure that it was my nerves and the thought of me going up against Mannie.

When Corey found out I was pregnant, he promised to take care of me. He said he'd always be there for me and the baby no matter what. I believed him when he said it, but now it seemed as if it was all lies. How could Corey be selfish enough to send the mother of his unborn child into the middle of a war zone?

What the hell am I gonna do? I gave him my word and I couldn't go back. Besides, I was doing this for my family. Corey needed me and so did our baby. That's it. It was on and popping. I was ready to face Mannie. The only thing left to do was to wait for Corey to give me the word.

I tenderly rubbed my stomach with thoughts of my baby running through my head. Then I said a silent prayer and asked God to forgive me in advance for what I about to do because deep inside I knew somebody was going to die.

Corey

I woke up around six thirty and was out of Brandi's house by seven. I had a million missed calls and even more text messages. After skimming through my phone's display, I realized most of the notifications were from Yvette. In all the time we'd been apart she hadn't called that much so I figured something had to be wrong. Even though I was hesitant to do so, I finally called her back. She told me that she had moved into the apartment at The Sovereign and she needed me to come through as soon as possible. The urgency in her voice inclined me to agree. I told her I needed some time, but I'd come through.

I went back to my hotel room to shit, shower, and shave. Then I went down to the lobby to see if I could catch the last of the free breakfast. I moved about the area looking back and forth trying to figure out exactly what I wanted. There was fruit, cereal, scrambled eggs, bacon, biscuits and fresh batter to make waffles. I decided I wanted a little bit of everything. I grabbed a plate and piled it high with food. Then as I walked toward the waffle maker, I noticed a beautiful woman over by the orange juice. I had to stop and admire her sexiness. She wore a gorgeous, tight black dress that clung to all her curves. She was light skinned, with long neatly twisted dreadlocks. I can't even lie, my dude stood at full attention. I almost dropped my plate as my mind immediately went into a daydream about everything I wanted to do to her.

The old Corey would have added her to the roster. I knew I could have had her by the way she looked at me. But with all the drama going on in my life, I decided to pass. Shit, I couldn't take any more, so I took my plate to a table and wolfed down my food so I could go see Yvette on a full stomach.

I exited the hotel through the double doors in the back and hit the keyless entry to unlock the truck door and start the engine. I frowned a little as I approached, then my heart jumped out of my chest onto the ground. My Escalade was a wreck. Someone had keyed the letters D-A-D-D-Y into my candy paint. The leather seats had been cut, the headrests slashed, and the windshield had been crashed.

It could've only been one of two people: Felicia or Yvette, and I was on my way to see Yvette. I called Joe-Joe to come scoop me and had him drop me off at my old apartment to get my other car.

Yvette

Corey came through mad as hell, talking some stuff about his Escalade being vandalized. It almost seemed like he was trying to accuse me of doing something so petty, but I wasn't trying to hear that. I told him if he would stay his ass out all of all them hoes' faces that shit like that wouldn't happen to him. I didn't have time to deal with Corey's drama. I needed him to calm down so I could talk to him about what Shawn had done to me. I also wanted to make sure he was good because I needed him to cover the rent at this high ass apartment.

Corey told me he was going to handle Shawn and promised me that I never had to worry about that nigga putting his hands on me again. He said he was going to pay the rent and bills at the apartment but then made some lame excuse about why he wouldn't be moving in. It hurt my feelings because I expected that we would make up and he would move into this space like we'd planned before I fought Felicia at the mall. I didn't understand why he was punishing me. Hell, Felicia threw the first blow; I was just defending myself. Corey said it was just too much right now and he wanted to be fair and give Felicia time to get used the idea of me and him. I pretended that I believed him, but something wasn't right. There was more to the story than Corey let on and it was now my job to find out exactly what it was.

Brandi

I found myself headed to Mannie's strip club in the most revealing outfit I could find. Even though I was barely dressed, I still found a way to look classy because I heard that Mannie wasn't into sleazy looking women. Thank God for good genes because even though I was right at two months pregnant, I still didn't have a big pooch. I inhaled deeply and said another silent prayer before I opened the door and made my way into the club.

A cloud of smoke hit me in the face and I was instantly sick from the mixed smells of men's' cologne, stripper perfume, and weed. I felt so out of place with music blaring from the speakers while beautiful, scantily clad women humped the air around their stripper poles. An insider told Corey that Mannie would be at the club tonight, so I scanned the room looking for him as I made my way to a table.

I didn't spot Mannie right away, but I did see a room full of other ballers who were popping bottles and littering the stage with singles from the wads of cash they were holding. This place was a gold digger's dream and I must say if I hadn't already trapped Corey with this baby, I think I could have found me a sucker in here tonight.

A half-naked waitress came over and asked if she could get me a drink. I ordered a virgin daiquiri that I could sip so I wouldn't look out of place. The waitress frowned until I handed her a 100-dollar bill and told her to keep the change. She walked away smiling and returned shortly with my drink.

Two hours and three non-alcoholic beverages later, I finally spotted Mannie. As expected he was surrounded by a crew of niggas and females. Once I saw him, it hit me that I didn't really have a plan. Somehow, some way I was supposed to make Mannie notice me without it being obvious that's what I was trying to do. I don't know why, but I hadn't counted on him having an entourage of people close to him. I sat at the table nursing my drink as I tried to come up with a clever way to bump into Mannie. I couldn't think of anything and was about ready to go, when I noticed him leave the VIP area headed for the men's restroom. I bee lined it to the bar area so I could watch the bathroom out of my peripheral vision. There was no real plan. All I knew to do was nonchalantly get in his path when he exited the men's room and hope he noticed me. Who am I kidding? I knew for a fact he would notice me. I'm gorgeous. Men always paid attention to my assets.

When Mannie finally came out of the restroom, I slid my slick ass right into the middle of the path he was taking back to the VIP. The crowd was dense so he couldn't move fast. I parked myself in the thickest part of the mob of partygoers and the next time Mannie stopped, I was right in front of him. I accidently (on purpose) rubbed my plump, bubble-shaped ass against his hand and turned around as if I were appalled that he'd touch my behind.

The look on my face was priceless. I should have been up for an academy award the way I played that role.

"Oh. I'm sorry, beautiful," he said, coyly. "I didn't try to do that. It's overly crowded in here and I... I..." Mannie stuttered.

It was funny to see him at a loss for words in his own establishment. Hell, that could only mean one thing: that he was enamored by my presence.

"No worries, handsome," I said with a wink of my left eye. "My name is Brandi. And you are?"

"Mannie," he answered extending his hand.

"Nice to meet you Mannie," I said seductively and pulled him in for a hug.

Mannie didn't resist my advance. In fact, when he hugged me, he held me just a smidgen longer than he should have. It was at that moment that I knew I had him hook, line, and sinker.

Corey

Brandi had been messing with Mannie tough for a couple of weeks. He'd been texting and calling late nights and begging to take her out. It almost made me jealous. I was a little territorial with my women. But I kept my focus and encouraged her to flirt with him and lead him on. There were a few nights that she cried to me because she wasn't attracted to him and she said she didn't want this to come down to her having to sleep with him.

Finally, the time came when I was ready to put my plan in motion so I told Brandi to invite Mannie over. I told her the only way we could pull this off is if she could convince him to come to her place. She was hesitant and mad as hell. She started screaming on me about how she was the mother of my child and how I should be protecting her and not putting her in the middle of this thing I have with Mannie. And even though I still wasn't sure the baby was mine, I lied to her again, promising her that once this situation was over with this nigga that we could be a family. I don't know why the promise of family worked on these women, but it always did.

It made me a little sad to know that I was going to have to break her heart when this was over. Shit, I was going to be there for my child, but I couldn't choose Brandi over Yvette or Felicia. My mind was in a whirlwind because I had all this trouble happening with the two women I really loved and I still hadn't made a decision who I really wanted to be with. Felicia had been down with me for so long, but Yvette came in and swept me off my feet. She was so different than everyone else and I knew I couldn't live without her.

I worked on Brandi for a little while longer.   I did that sex thing to her again. She stopped crying and agreed to be my ride or die. Then she picked up the phone and texted Mannie.

Brandi

In the name of love and for the sake of my unborn child, I went along with Corey's request. Inviting Mannie over was the easy part. Since the day I met him, he'd been begging to come to my place for a "Netflix and chill" date, so I put the plan in motion. I sent him a one-word text with a private invitation to my apartment.

Me: Netflix?

Mannie: When?

Me: Tomorrow night bout ten.

Mannie: I'm there!

I didn't fully know the plan when I set it in motion. All I knew was that Joe-Joe would be waiting for Mannie when he got there.

****

The following night, Mannie hit me up right around nine-thirty and asked for the address to my apartment. Corey had told me to keep him on the phone while he drove. That would give us a one up on Mannie because I was supposed to text Joe-Joe the moment Mannie pulled up into my complex.

Corey told me to hang up with Mannie once I notified Joe-Joe. Then I was supposed to go into my back bedroom and wait until Corey let me know it was safe to come out. My pounding heart kept me from being able to sit still, so I stood at my door and looked out the peephole. I looked out just in time to see Joe-Joe move down the hallway. He tucked himself on the blind side of the stairwell and waited for Mannie to walk up. Then I saw Mannie walking down the hall toward my place with an air of cockiness about him. Before he could knock on my front door, Joe-Joe came rushing toward him with a gun. I covered my mouth to hold in the squeal. I don't know why I was surprised to see the gun, but it startled me. My heart beat faster. I was immediately upset with myself for getting involved. This had gone far enough and I just wanted it to be over.

With my eyeballs glued to the peephole, I saw Mannie turn around abruptly. He grabbed for the gun that Joe-Joe had and they started to scuffle. Not long after, I heard a gunshot. Then another. After which, I felt the worst pain of my life in my abdomen. The burning sensation had me in agony. I grabbed my stomach and felt a warm gushy flow, then fell to my knees before screaming for help. I crawled in the bathroom to get a towel to cover the wound before it hit me that I was holding my cell phone. I dialed 911 and begged them to get an ambulance to my place as quickly as possible. I didn't know or care what had happened with Joe-Joe or Mannie. I just lay on the floor praying that the paramedics would show up in time to save me as my life flashed quickly before my eyes. Then I passed out.

Yvette

It was one in the morning and I was laying in the living room of our apartment in a pink t-shirt and a pair of white lace boy short panties. For some reason, I couldn't sleep. Corey was on my mind heavy and I lay in the front, hoping he would come in tonight. When this thing started with me and Corey, I thought it would be different. But here I was, yet again, up at night waiting on a nigga to come home to me, just like I had done with Shawn.

I flicked through Instagram trying to curb my thoughts of Corey and pass some time. I found myself on THESHADEROOMINC, mindlessly checking out the unnecessary back and forth between 50 Cent and Rick Ross' old asses. I couldn't make sense of what was happening between them but reading the comments was helping to keep my mind off of Corey.

Just as my eyes got heavy and I started to doze off, I heard pounding on the front door. I put my phone down, stood up from the couch, and tip-toed quietly toward the door. I veered out the peephole and saw the top of Corey's head. I momentarily wondered why he didn't just use his key to come inside, but before I could think too long, he started beating on the door again. This time he yelled for me to hurry up and open the door.

"Oh my God, Corey! What happened to you?" I yelled when he crossed the threshold into the apartment.

Corey staggered into the living room without saying a word. He was covered in blood from head to toe. He pushed past me, headed straight for the bathroom.

"Corey, baby! What happened? Are you okay?" I asked in a panic.

"Hell no, I'm not okay. Them niggas killed Joe-Joe!" He screamed.

"Oh no baby! You can't be serious! How did that happen? Have you been shot? Do we need to go to the hospital?" I was really concerned that he'd been hit. As he moved about the bathroom touching things, he left bloodstains everywhere.

"Calm down! I'm not hurt. That's all Joe-Joe's blood. I need to jump in the shower and wash up, then I have to hit the streets and handle this shit! Now leave me alone so I can get done."

Brandi

I woke up in a hospital bed surrounded by family, friends, and get well balloons. I was in an extreme amount of pain, but the warmth of my mother's hands as she held mine was all the comfort I needed. I blinked a few times to gain focus before I noticed the look in my mother's eyes. I opened my mouth to speak, but the words wouldn't come. I scanned the room again and saw my sister, Donna sitting solemnly in a chair in the corner. I was livid! Strength came from nowhere!

"Get that bitch out of here," I screamed, but nobody moved. "I mean it! Get her out of here right now or I will get up and put her out myself."

My grandmother came toward me. "Calm down baby. Now is not the time. We almost lost you. Do you understand that? There are bigger things to worry about." My grandmother fell to her knees and began to pray. I loved and respected her so much that I closed my eyes and allowed her to pray.

When she finished, my sister walked over to me and kissed my forehead. "I love you Brandi and I'm sorry that you lost your baby. We will get through this…"

I didn't hear anything after she said I'd lost my baby. My ears went deaf, my eyes blind and my body numb. The only part of me that moved was the stream of tears down my face. Just when I thought things couldn't get any worse, two detectives walked into my room and demanded that my family leave because they wanted to talk to me about the shooting.

Corey

A few hours after I left Yvette, I sat quietly on the edge of my hotel bed staring at the white walls. I couldn't believe Joe-Joe had been killed and the rage inside of me was growing stronger and stronger. My mind raced. I wanted to go out and kill every nigga responsible, but I knew I had to be smart. I got word that Brandi had been shot and was in the hospital. I wanted to go see her too, but I knew I had to lay low. I didn't want to be associated with the shooting at all and I only hoped she would be smart enough not to talk to the cops when they came sniffing around.

Two days passed and I was still at the hotel. I sat up in the bed as the moon's rays peeked through the hotel room shades. I hadn't slept a wink. All I could do was try to find some comfort in the bottle of Apple Crown I'd been sipping on and the blunts I'd smoked back to back. This beef with Mannie had become costly and for the first time in a long time I was stumped. I didn't know what to do or where to turn. All I knew for sure was that somehow, some way, I had to find my way out of this mess without going to prison. There was no way I could go to jail and leave my son behind.

Finally, around 4:00 AM, sleep started to catch up to me. My eyes got heavy and I leaned back onto the bed. I didn't know if I was tripping or not, but just as I started to doze off, I thought I heard heavy footsteps coming down the hallway. Then it turned to sounds of running and that bothered me because I'd paid for every room on the floor just to be sure I would be alone. As the sound got louder and louder, I was beyond nervous.

I turned out all the lights in my suite, then ran to the closet and frantically rummaged through my duffel bag for .45 caliber handgun that I never left home without. Something was off and I had to be ready just in case some of Mannie's goons were coming for me.

I suddenly heard knocking on the room door. Instinctively I walked toward the door to open it before I stopped in my tracks and came to my senses. The knocking turned to banging. I panicked, cocked the gun and pointed it at the door as I tip-toed toward it. Once I was close enough to look through the peephole, I lowered my gun and opened the door.

"Yvette! What the hell are you doing here? You scared the shit out of me," I said as I raised the gun to show her the danger she'd put herself in by surprising me.

She pushed her way past me and into the room without speaking. She closed the door and locked it. That's when I noticed the tears and heavy breathing.

Then she started screaming. "Oh my gosh baby! I have been calling you! Your phone is going straight to voicemail."

"Calm down. I'm trying to lay low and you're going to bring heat being all extra. Here I am in some real shit and you have the nerve to come at me with this BS about me not answering the phone. Go home Yvette. I don't have time for this!"

"Two Spanish guys came to the apartment, Corey. They tried to break in! I was so scared that I didn't know what to do. I called you over and over but you never answered. I needed you Corey!"

"Wait! What do you mean someone tried to break in? Are you ok? What happened?" My tone had softened and I put the gun down on the table. It upset me that I'd gotten my sweetheart caught up in the middle of this mess. It felt like my world had flipped upside down.

I pulled her close and hugged her tight as she cried on my shoulder. She was so nervous as she talked that I could feel her body tremble as I held her. Unbelievably, she'd hid in the closet, clutching the .22 caliber pistol that I'd left there for her protection. The guys turned the house upside down, looking in every nook and cranny for something. Before they got to the closet and found her, one of the guys got a phone call that made them leave.

I breathed a sigh of relief and told Yvette not to go back to the house until after I could send a few of my boys to go by there and check it out. I told her that she could stay with me for just one night, then we'd find a safe place for her to hang out until I could line this mess out.

I looked down at Yvette. In a daze, I stared at her. She was scared but she trusted me. In that moment, she became the most beautiful girl in the world. I held her just a little bit tighter. She moved toward me and sensually licked her lips. My man started to swell. Now didn't seem like the time, but she was getting hard to resist. She tiptoed and pressed her soft lips against mine. I grabbed her and carried her over to the bed. She looked up at me and arched her back. I gently caressed her and tenderly unbuttoned her shirt. She moaned as I released both of her swollen breasts from her bra and moved my body between her thighs. I put in work until we both exploded, then after washing up I fell into a very deep sleep.

Brandi

After the detectives abruptly removed my family from my hospital room, they immediately began with their good cop and bad cop routine. I had seen enough *Law and Order* to know what the hell they were up to.

"Ma'am. I know that this isn't the best time or circumstances to speak with you, but we really need some information and we think that you can help," the good cop said. "My name is Detective Davenport and this is my partner, Detective Luis."

I looked at them with the reminisce of tears still in my eyes. "Look. I don't know if they told you, but I just found out I lost my baby. I don't know what you want from me. I didn't see anything. Just in case you haven't noticed, I am the innocent victim here." I lapped my eyes at the both of them.

Then, the bad cop, Detective Luis stepped in. "We don't have time to play games young lady. We are aware you know more than what you say you do," he said as he reached in his back pocket and pulled out a plastic bag with the word "EVIDENCE" written on it.

"I was in my house watching an *Empire* marathon. The next thing I knew, I was shot through my door. So, what could possibly know?" I smirked. These clowns started to pluck my last nerves. One thing I knew from growing up on the streets, you don't snitch.

Detective Luis looked at me with a similar smirk on his face. He was a cocky bitch.

"Can you explain this?" He asked as he pulled out what looked like a napkin from the plastic bag.

My eyes got big. It definitely was a napkin. It was also tainted with blood. "I can't read it," I lied.

He put it closer to my face so I could get a good look. It read: 356 Mockingbird Lane, Apt. B, 10 o'clock.

"Well, Brandi. Is this your address or not?" Detective Luis yelled.

I looked at him. I tried not to show the fear that was engulfing my body. I remained silent.

"Answer the question, Brandi," said Detective Davenport in a more soothing voice.

"Yes. It is my address. Now what? Maybe I dropped it in the walkway or something," I said sarcastically.

The detectives looked at each other. It was that "I got you now" look.

Detective Luis put the napkin back in the plastic evidence bag. "We found this on one of the victims. It was in his pocket."

I felt sick to the stomach. I immediately leaned over my bed and vomited on the floor. It missed Detective Luis' shoes by mere millimeters. I secretly pushed the nurse's button. The nurse ran into the room.

"What's wrong, Brandi," she said.

"I am feeling really sick," I responded.

She turned to the detectives and advised them that they needed to leave. I looked at them both as they walked out of the door. I knew that I had gotten myself into some shit. "Where is Corey's ass when I need him the most?" I thought to myself.

After the nurse finished checking my vitals, I looked at the clock on the wall. It was almost midnight. I could not believe that another day had gone by and I still hadn't heard from Corey. I took a bullet for his ass and he didn't have the common courtesy to at least call. The more I thought about it, the angrier I got. I picked up the phone and dialed his number. I dialed his number back to back at least four or five times. His phone just kept going to voicemail. After the last attempt, I decided to leave a message.

"Corey. Where in the hell are you? I am laid up in the hospital after taking a bullet for your ass. You ain't have the damn decency enough to call. Shit, if you don't give a fuck about me, at least you could call to find out how your baby is doing. You need to call me now. I am in Methodist Hospital, Room 2032."

I click the END button on my cell and burst into tears. I cried like a damn baby. As much as I wanted Corey and I to be together, I couldn't shake the feeling that he was just using me. I swear if I find out that nigga used me and I lost my baby as a result of it, there will definitely be hell to pay. I knew my phone had not rung, but I checked it one more time anyway. No missed calls. "Corey, where are you," I thought before falling fast asleep.

Gina

It was ten o'clock in the morning and I was already pouring my fourth glass of wine. I hadn't heard from Corey since the night he kicked me out of his hotel room and it was bothering me bad. All kinds of thoughts ran through my head. I questioned myself over and over. *Why did I ask him to make love to me? Why did I let my feelings get the best of me? Why didn't I just go with the flow so I could keep Corey in my life? We had a good thing and I had to go and fuck it up, all because I caught feelings when I wasn't supposed to.*

But then again, why was it wrong for me to love Corey? He had all these expectations of me. I couldn't post pictures of us on social media. I couldn't have other niggas in the house or he refused to pay the rent. I couldn't have male friends. I couldn't do a lot of things. I'd been faithful to this man for more than two years and he had a live in girlfriend the entire time. It pissed me off to no end to think that Corey felt so entitled to control my life without giving me anything but sex and rent money in return. I was a good girl. I deserved to be loved. I deserved to have a man to come home to at night. I deserved for Corey to treat me right.

All the thoughts of Corey and how he'd treated me flooded my brain. My head started to feel like someone was beating it with a hammer. Immediately, I jumped up from the sofa and practically ran to the laundry room. I grabbed two bottles of bleach and made a beeline to the bathroom. Once there, I filled the bathtub halfway with water. Then I stood and stared. I was so angry at Corey that I couldn't move for a few minutes. Once I snapped back, I rushed into my bedroom to the dresser. I opened the drawer where Corey kept his things. I pulled out all the Polo underwear and expensive Stance socks, then I went to the closet and grabbed the designer jeans, shirts, and hats. He didn't keep many things at my apartment, but it gave me pleasure to give a bleach bath to any and every thing that I could get my hands on.

It was the wee hours of the morning by the time I pulled myself together. I was still in the bathroom. The smell of bleach permeated the air. I'd been in there sitting on the floor crying for hours. My mind wouldn't give me any peace. I couldn't put my finger on why I loved Corey so much and I definitely didn't understand how or why I'd pretended not to love him for so long. I guess deep down inside I knew I was just a jump off. I knew his main attraction to me was the thought that there were no strings attached, but I secretly hoped that one day he would come to his senses and see me for the woman that I am.

I got up and pulled the stopper from the tub. After I lugged Corey's fully-bleached, soaking wet clothes to the kitchen trash, I went back to the bathroom and turned on the shower. I adjusted the water to steaming hot, climbed in and scrubbed my body all over. It felt good to wash off all the negative energy and watch it spiral down the drain. When I finished, I crawled into my bed and cried myself to sleep... again.

The next morning, the burning sensation of vomit in the back of my throat woke me. I hustled to the bathroom for release. I could still smell the scent of bleach lingering in the air. I heaved some more until there was nothing left. Instantly, I regretted drinking all of that wine on an empty stomach. My mind started to race again. I called Corey, but he didn't answer. I called ten times in a row. Still no answer. I was livid. Corey had hurt me for the first and last time and he was going to pay. All I had to do was devise a plan.

Brandi

"Alright Ms. Knight, here are your discharge papers," the nurse said. "Your doctor would like to see you back in about two weeks."

I shook my head and smiled. The only thing that was on my mind was finding out what was going on with Corey.

"She will be there. I will make sure of it," my sister Donna said.

Donna had been by my side since the day I was admitted to the hospital. As much as I wanted to continue to be angry with her, I just couldn't. God definitely worked in mysterious ways. It was a shame that it took a near death experience for us to come back together. We promised each other we would never let a man come between us again.

The drive home was sort of quiet. I was sure Donna could tell that something was bothering me. I noticed how she continued to peep at me out the corner of her eyes. Finally, she said, "Brandi, what really happened?"

"I don't want to talk about it right now," I responded.

I thought that would put an end the questioning, but of course it didn't.

"I know we have just started to get back on good terms, but now that you are back in my life, I don't want to lose you. If you have gotten yourself caught up in something serious, I want to help you get out of it. You have to trust me," she sincerely said, while grabbing my hand and squeezing it tight.

I started to tear up at the fact my sister still cared enough about me to put herself in the middle of some shit I wished I hadn't gotten myself in to begin with.

"I know. I am so sorry it took this to bring us back together again, but I think it's best that you don't get involved. I have to take care of this myself.

Just then, my cell phone rang. I hoped it was Corey, but it wasn't. However, I immediately recognized the voice. "Hello Detective Davenport. How may I help you?"

"Detective Luis and I stopped by the hospital and they advised us that you were discharged about an hour ago. We were hoping that you could stop by the police station. We still have some unanswered questions that we hoped you could help us with," he said.

I looked at my sister. "I told you before. I don't have any more answers. Plus, I am on my way to my mother's house. I don't have time to come down to the station," I said with irritation in my voice. Donna glanced over at me.

"I am trying to be very patient with you, but you are making it very difficult. I was hoping you would come voluntarily. Let me say this, if you don't come down to the station today, then we will have no choice but to put a warrant out for your arrest."

My heart dropped to the bottom of my gut. "A warrant for my arrest," I yelled. "For what?"

"We believe that you are withholding information about a murder case. This alone gives us the right to bring you in, voluntarily or involuntarily, to question you. It's up to you how you want to do this," Detective Davenport stated.

I could hear Detective Luis in the background. "She can either do this the easy way or the hard way."

I conceded. "Okay. I can be there in about twenty minutes." I hung up the phone.

I looked at Donna and said, "I need to tell you something." She pulled into the Exxon gas station and parked the car.

"I'm listening," she said.

I told her everything. I started from the beginning. She looked at me like she couldn't believe what I was telling her. I finished by asking, "Can you go with me to the police station? They want to ask me more questions."

"No," she said. "We will not go to the police station without our lawyer." She pressed the auto-dial on her phone. A male voice bellowed through the radio speakers in the car.

"What's up babe?" the voice asked.

"It's my sister. She's in trouble. Can you meet us at the police station in twenty minutes?" Donna pleaded.

"I'll be there in ten," he replied.

Donna pulled out of the gas station and headed to the police station.

"Sister, who was that?" I quizzed.

She looked at me and smiled. "It's my fiancé. He is also happens to be one of the best damn defense attorneys in town."

Yvette

The next morning, I got up and left the hotel before Corey awoke. Even though I was still on that sex high, I was mad and disappointed in myself that I'd let him foil my plan. I went to the room to see if I could seduce him into telling me the truth about what had happened when Joe-Joe was killed because I knew he hadn't told me the everything. I completely made up that story about the Hispanic dudes breaking in to see if I could get anything out of him, but it didn't work. Instead, I was the one who got seduced.

I knew I couldn't go back to the apartment because he had sent some of his boys there to hang around just in case things heated up again. As I drove around the block several times, it suddenly hit me that my grandmother lived in the vicinity. I hadn't talked to her in a long while so I busted a U-Turn and headed her way. Grammy, as we called her, was old school. I knew for a fact she was going to cuss me up one side and down the other for coming by without calling. But I didn't mind. That was always how she rolled. If Grammy didn't cuss you out, then she didn't love you. I grinned just a little at the thought of seeing her. That smile quickly faded when I looked in the rear view mirror and saw flashing lights.

Blue and white flashing lights meant one thing only. Police! And I didn't have time for that bullshit. I grabbed my phone to call Corey. I wanted to let him know I was being pulled over just in case I needed him or anybody else for that matter. These days a simple traffic stop could be a matter of life and death when you are guilty of

DWB- *driving while black*. Of course, he didn't answer! "Why can't he just be here when I need him?" I asked myself as I pulled over into the parking lot of an upcoming gas station.

I sat straight up in my seat with both hands resting visibly on top of the steering wheel. My heart beat erratically out of my chest. I took three deep breaths to help calm myself and waited for the cop to approach my vehicle. After a few minutes of sitting, I slightly raised my head to try and catch a glimpse of the officer in my rearview mirror. "What the hell is he doing back there?" I mumbled. Finally, I could see him leave his patrol car to approach the vehicle. I breathed a slight sigh of relief when I saw he was black. I understood that I wasn't completely in the clear, but I didn't feel like I'd be the victim of a hate crime in the form of police brutality.

He was a handsome man. If I was even a slightly attractive woman, I would have tried to put the moves on him. But since I was just plain ole Yvette, I decided to keep it cool and see where this went. Maybe he'd give me a warning for that illegal U-turn and send me on my way.

"License and registration, please Ma'am."

"Yes sir," I said as I grabbed the registration from my glove box. "My license is in my purse in the back seat. May I get it?" I asked gesturing toward it before I moved.

He nodded his approval and then I grabbed my license from the wallet in my purse and handed both items to the officer. He took them and told me not to move, then he walked back to his patrol car.

After fifteen minutes of anxiously waiting, I noticed a black on black Chevy Tahoe pull up. I knew immediately that it was an unmarked police vehicle, but I couldn't for the life of me figure out why the hell an unmarked car had arrived.

"What can I do for you?" I asked as soon as the two detectives who'd gotten out of the Tahoe approached my vehicle.

"We'll be asking the questions," the shorter one of them said. I guess he was supposed to be the bad cop. If I wasn't scared, I would have laughed in his face because that good cop, bad cop routine was so played out. Besides, I still had no clue why two detectives were coming for me so I kept my cool.

The taller one stuck his hand out and flashed a half smiled at me. "My name is Detective Davenport and this is my partner, Detective Luis."

"Okay," I said nervously and extended my hand to him as well. "May I ask a question, Detective Davenport?"

He nodded, so I proceeded to talk. "Why are two detectives necessary when all I did was make an illegal U-turn? I have a valid driver's license, along with my insurance and registration. What is this about?"

"My partner and I are homicide detectives. We are investigating the murder of Joseph Mitchell and we think you may have some information that could help us move this case along."

My eyebrows wormed toward each other. "There has to be some sort of mix up, sir. I don't know anybody who has been murdered. And I definitely don't know a Joseph Mitchell."

Then it hit me. Joe-Joe. Damn!

Gina

I couldn't believe that Corey still wasn't answering my calls. At this point, I knew I'd left over fifty messages on Corey's cell phone. I was fed up with him, but I couldn't get him off of my mind. I couldn't concentrate on anything, but him. It was so bad, I called my job and made up a lie about why I couldn't report to work. I knew if I went in, it would just end in disaster. I went to my fridge and grabbed my bottle of Goose. Instead of getting a shot glass like I normally would, I turned the bottle up to my head and gulped it down like spring water. The sensation went straight to my head. I walked over to the couch and sat down. It seemed like the room was spinning. I attempted to call Corey again. I left another voice message.

"Corey. I've called you so many times, I don't know the count anymore. I know you don't want me to just show up at your front door. Do you? Look. Dammit. Just answer your phone. We need to talk," I slurred as I left my final message.

I gave him an hour to call me back. Two hours had passed. I knew it was time for me to stop moping around this house. I got up and took a cold shower to help me sober up. I had decided to confront Corey's ass.

"I know that I am a quality bitch. I am just as worthy of his attention and love as Felicia is," I mumbled out loud. "He will not deny me. He will love me!" I took the pictures that I had shredded into tiny pieces and placed them neatly inside my ashtray. I grabbed my lighter, set the shreds on fire, and marveled in delight as I watched it burn.

Corey

When I opened my eyes from sleeping, I noticed Yvette was long gone. I wasn't really feeling the fact that she had just bounced on me like that, but I couldn't worry too much about it. I had bigger fish to fry. I stepped out of bed and shuttered a little bit when my bare feet hit the cold floor. I rummaged around for a second until I found my house shoes and slid them on. Then I yawned, stretched, and went to the bathroom to take care of my morning business.

After taking a piss and brushing my teeth, I walked out of the bathroom across the room and grabbed my phone. I'd been incognito for a few days so it was time for me to make some moves. I ain't gone lie. I was a little vexed about getting back out in the streets before that shit with Joe-Joe and Mannie was calm. But that money wasn't going to make itself, so I powered my phone up. My text message and voicemail icons instantly flickered. I had more than 250 text messages and 50 voicemails and the majority of them were from Yvette, Brandi, and Gina. I shook my head in disbelief. Who the fuck had time to call me repeatedly like that? This situation with these women was becoming too much. I had to hurry up and find a way to get myself out of this.

I rubbed my temples and then walked to the closet and grabbed my bag. I had rolled a couple of blunts the night before so I pulled one out and lit it. I took a few drags then moved toward the hotel window and stared out. I rubbed my chin and smoked. Weed always helped me think. Before I could make up my mind on what to do, my phone started to vibrate in my hands. I looked down at the caller ID. It was Felicia. My heart pounded a little bit. My hands were sweating. I contemplated answering the phone and decided to let it go. I put the blunt out in an ashtray that was sitting on the table by the window. Then I went and sat back down on the bed.

I couldn't believe Felicia was calling. I hadn't heard from her in weeks. Somewhere deep in the back of my mind, I hoped she had moved on. But that would have been too easy. Nothing in my life ever went smoothly so I knew she was still waiting for me to come back.

The phone buzzed again. This time it was Yvette. I sent her ass to voicemail. Shit, if she really wanted to talk, she shouldn't have left the room before I got up. I decided it was time for me to check on Brandi. I was ready to see her, so I dialed her number to let her know I was going to swing through. I figured I'd better try to get to her before the cops did, plus I wanted to make sure everything was good with her pregnancy. I was finally getting used to the idea of having a son. I sat patiently waiting while the phone rang. I was shocked and pissed when she didn't pick up. How the hell did she feel blowing me up for days then not answering when I called? I hung up and dialed again. I got an answer on the first ring, but it wasn't Brandi.

"Hello," a male voice boomed through the speaker of my cell phone. I took the phone from my ear and looked at the caller ID to be sure I'd dialed the right number. I scratched my head. Brandi's number was on the screen, but a man was on the other end of the line.

"Who the fuck is this?" I roared. "Put Brandi on the phone!"

"Corey. This is Detective Luis. If you want to talk to Brandi, I suggest you come down to the precinct…"

I hung up before that pig could finish his sentence. He had me all the way messed up if he thought I was ever going to willingly step foot in a police station. I couldn't believe they had Brandi. I had to find a way to get her away from there before she gave me up. There was only one other person I figured we could trust to help us, so I decided to call Brandi's sister Donna. Of course they were beefing, but I knew they still loved each other and Donna wouldn't want to see her younger sister locked up on some murder shit so I hit her up.

I dialed Donna twice. I didn't get an answer either time. Before I could make my third attempt, my phone was buzzing again. It was Felicia. I didn't want to talk but I accidently hit accept when I was trying to decline the call.

"Damn!" I said aloud before I put the phone to my ear.

"Hello." I was real dry with my greeting. Hell, I loved Felicia but I had too much going on and my love life with her was last on the list of priorities for today.

"Corey! I'm glad you answered. I know you've been avoiding me because you think I'm calling to talk about us. But that's not the case. I wanted to let you know that two detectives have been snooping around asking questions about you. I don't know what's going on but they said Joe-Joe is dead. Please tell me it's not true Corey! Come see me. I need to know what's happening."

Felicia was yelling and sobbing uncontrollably into the phone. She'd known Joe-Joe as long as I had. I wanted to comfort her and tell her that it wasn't true. But I knew I couldn't do that. Somewhere deep inside though, I couldn't bring myself to say the words aloud that my cousin and best friend was dead, especially since he died on my watch and I hadn't got them niggas back yet.

"Listen, Felicia. Calm down. We can't be talking on the phone. Them folks might be listening. I tell you what I am going to do. I will meet up with you at our spot. Not today though. I will let you know when. Just stay alert and ready. Don't talk to the detectives at all. Please, baby. Ok?"

She sniffled a few times before answering. "Ok. Corey. Just please let me know something soon."

"I will get with you later. I have to go now, but I promise you I will be in touch soon."

"Ok. Bye Corey," she said preparing to disconnect the call.

"Felicia," I called out before she hung up.

"Yes, Corey?"

"I love you girl. I always have and I always will. Remember that, ok? No matter what happens. I love you, always." Then I hung up before she could respond.

Brandi

I was extremely nervous as we pulled into the parking lot of the police station. My sister promised me I had absolutely nothing to worry about. Her lawyer fiancé was supposed to be the best in town. Although I had no clue who he was, I had no choice but to trust my sister.

We were only in the parking lot for a couple of minutes before a black, Lexus IS 200 pulled in the parking space beside us. Donna and I got out of the car. At the same time, Donna's fiancé got out too. I had to do a double take. Given the circumstances, gawking at this man and admiring how absolutely handsome he was should have been the last thing on my mind. "Damn. Where in the hell did you find him," I asked Donna as we walked around the car to greet him.

"Carmelo. This is my sister Brandi. Brandi, this is my fiancé Carmelo Montiago," Donna said as she introduced us.

I stood there for a second just gazing into his eyes. I couldn't help it. He was so handsome. "Way more handsome than Corey," I thought to myself.

"Hello. It's nice to finally meet you. It's unfortunate that it had to be under these circumstances," Carmelo said as he extended his hand to shake mine.

As we walked towards the entrance of the precinct, I gave him the abbreviated version of what happened. "Do you think you can help me?"

He looked at my sister with a hint of trepidation and said, "I'm going to be honest with you. If everything you have told me is true, and I assume it is, then right now you are an accessory to murder." He fixed his tie as we prepared to enter the doors of the precinct. "That makes you just as much responsible for the murder of this young man as the person who pulled the trigger--even though your intent wasn't to kill Joe-Joe."

I took a deep breath as we walked into the main lobby of the precinct. Detective Luis was waiting. "I'm glad you made the decision to come in. It was in your best interest."

"Greetings Detective. I'm Carmelo Montiago. I am representing Mrs. Knight," Attorney Montiago boasted.

Detective Luis looked at Carmelo up and down. "Yeah. I know you. You're that hot shot defense attorney who takes pride in letting criminals walk the streets. Well, this time, you will have something on your hands. This case won't be so easy. So, I hope you are ready," he taunted.

"I'm always ready, Detective. Don't forget that Brandi and every other client I have ever represented is innocent until proven guilty. I trust you haven't convicted her before you know all the facts."

Detective Luis shook his head. "Follow me," he snarled.

Yvette

I'd had some pretty rough days in all my years of living, but the day that I was stopped by those detectives and forced to go to the police station was one of the worst. I couldn't stop reliving the moment that I watched Brandi through the two-way mirror with that fine ass high profile attorney. I knew exactly who Carmelo Montiago was the moment I laid eyes on him. But I also knew this was some deep shit if he was her lawyer.

I sat beside Detective Davenport for a couple of hours on the opposite side of the glass while Detective Luis prodded Brandi. He did everything he could to scare her into rolling over on Corey, but her lawyer kept shutting everything down. After all of that, the only thing she ever admitted was that she'd lost her unborn child as a result of the shooting and that Corey was the father of the baby.

When she said it, I didn't react. I knew the game these detectives were playing. They figured if they pissed me off bad enough then I would tell on Corey. So I kept my composure. Even though I was fuming on the inside, I didn't give Detective Davenport any indication that I was upset. He searched my face for an expression, I gave him nothing. After all I'd seen from them today, I knew two things for sure:

1. They didn't have any evidence that Corey had committed a crime and

2. I finally knew what Corey was hiding from me.

When I got up and excused myself from the interrogation room, Detective Davenport attempted to stop me, but I knew my rights so I kept right on stepping.

Now here I was hours later lying under an old fashioned quilt at my grandmother's house trying to forget what I'd seen and heard. I can't tell you enough how foolish I felt for trusting Corey. I wiped my eyes as the tears fell and asked myself if I really loved Corey. I couldn't believe all this drama was unfolding. I started to feel as if I should have just kept putting up with Shawn's mess.

I pulled the quilt back and sat up on the edge of the bed. Suddenly, I heard a loud rumbling sound in the driveway. I rushed to the window and saw my brother Jerome pulling up. The loud noise was him hitting my grandmother's trash can as he sped up the drive. I wasn't surprised to see him because Jerome was a little closer to my grandma than I was. He lived with her off and on when he was in between chics. For some reason that I have yet to understand, she always favored him. Which is probably the same reason he always stayed in trouble.

Not even a few minutes later I heard the loud bang of Grammy's front door being kicked open. At the same time, I heard her screaming and the police yelling.

"Freeze! Police! Get on the ground!"

I rushed out of the back bedroom to a mob of policemen moving about Grammy's small living room. Tears instantly welled in my eyes when I saw my seventy-five year old grandmother on the floor, face-down with her hands out in front of her and a rifle pressed into her back. Before I could react, another cop wrestled me to the floor and handcuffed me while the others ransacked the house.

"What's this about! Why are yall here?" I screamed frantically. I couldn't help but blame Corey for all of this. At this point, I wish I knew the truth about what had happened to Joe-Joe. I would have told it all. My Grammy didn't deserve to be caught up in all of this madness. I looked over at her. She was scared but calm. I could see it all in her eyes. She motioned to me to be quiet. So I complied.

The police continued to scramble through the house. One of them yelled, "Get him! He just ran out the back door!"

I couldn't see what was going on, but I heard a lot of shuffling and then the ferocious barking of a police K-9. All I could do was stay down and cry. I thought they were going to kill my brother.

The officers that were in the house with Grammy and me got a call on their radios stating that the suspect was in custody and they could release us. Several seconds later one of the officers grabbed me by my hair and pulled me up.

"Owwww!" I screamed out aloud. "What was that for?"

"Shut up and turn around so I can remove the cuffs," he responded angrily.

At the same time, another cop gently lifted Grammy from the

floor and apologized for busting in.

"Owwww!" I yelled again as the officer tightened the cuffs on my wrists.

Grammy was pissed. "Leave her alone, you fucking pig! You got the person you came for. Now release my granddaughter and get the hell out of my house!" She looked the evil officer directly in his eyes as she spoke.

"Calm down old lady or you will be next," he said as he turned the key in the handcuffs and let me go.

Finally, after they left, Grammy and I walked across her shabby wooden floor onto the creaky porch where we saw my brother Jerome being pushed into the back of the squad car. He looked up and caught eyes with Grammy, then mouthed the words "I'm sorry."

Corey

I dialed Yvette frantically. The detectives had contacted both Brandi and Felicia so it was a no brainer to me that they would try to find her, too.

"Damn!" I said when she didn't answer. I was feeling nervous but I didn't want to panic. This situation was getting out of hand. I had left the hotel so I could link up with the niggas I needed to see to keep my money flowing, but dodging these detectives and keeping my girls safe had become my main focus.

I whipped the car around toward the place I shared with Yvette. I didn't see her car. I walked in the door and caught the reminisce of her sweet scent. I immediately had a flashback to the first time I met her in the club. As much as I didn't want to admit it, Yvette had my heart. "Shake that shit off," I thought out loud. I had business to handle. When it came to these streets, the minute you let feelings take over, was the minute you die. I walked in her bedroom. It was perfect. A clear indication that Yvette had not been staying at the house. For Yvette to be a woman, she cared more about a clean car than a clean house.

I pulled out my cell and called Tony. I sent Tony to the house after Yvette said two Spanish dudes ran up in the apartment. "What up doe," I said when he answered.

The first thing out of his mouth was, "Yo man. I am sorry to hear about your kid. I don't know what I would do if Keisha told me she lost our lil nigga."

My heart dropped. "What da fuck you mean lost--my son dead? Is that what the fuck you saying to me?"

Tony was quiet. All I could hear were gulps. "Damn. I thought you knew."

"Naw dawg. I haven't talked to Brandi since the shooting," I responded.

I wasn't sure about much of anything anymore, but just when I finally accepted that I was going to have me a seed, this punk ass nigga tells me he dead. I couldn't believe I let Brandi go into a situation that put the life of my unborn child in jeopardy. Especially hearing that my son had paid the price. I needed to get to Brandi. I wasn't there when the mother of my unborn child needed me the most. I knew she blamed me. Shit, I blamed me. I just didn't know if she was angry enough to tell the cops what really happened. I grabbed a couple of things from my closet. I went to the fridge, grabbed a Coke, snatched my keys from the breakfast bar and left. I needed to get back to the hotel so I could regroup.

As I drove down the road, my head was on a swivel. It felt like I was being followed. It seemed like all eyes were on me. I was paranoid. Then, my phone rang. It was Yvette. I let it go to voicemail. She followed up with a 911 text. She texted me again.

"The cops just picked up my brother. Call me. Or, I'm going to--."

My phone went dead before I could finish reading what the fuck she was going to do! *Shit.*

Gina

It's like the world had gone mad around me and I had gone mad with it. It was six in the morning and I was up for no reason at all. I hadn't been to work in days because I couldn't focus on anything but Corey. When I got tired of making excuses to my boss, I put in for two weeks of vacation to give myself time to regroup. I'd cried myself all out. I was no longer hurt, now I was just pissed off.

I took a washcloth from the towel rack and washed the sleep from my eyes, then stood staring at myself in the mirror. My hair was all over my head. I'd rocked bedhead for at least five days. Dark circles adorned my eyes. I was only twenty-seven and I had a crease in the middle of my forehead. A wrinkle? Corey was killing me. I wondered where things had gone wrong.

I thought I had the perfect plan to get Corey. My homegirl Tracy had nabbed her man, Deondre, by pretending like she didn't want anything serious from him. She promised me the shit would work with me and Corey, but obviously she was wrong. I shook my head to snap myself out of the trance I was falling into, then reached down for my toothbrush to get the icky taste from my mouth. I couldn't have been paying attention because as I wet it and slapped on the toothpaste, I noticed that I had picked up the spare that Corey kept in my bathroom for all the late nights and early mornings we spent. Instead of putting it back in the holder, I used it. I savored every minute and smiled at the thought of Corey's DNA swishing around in my mouth. When I was done, I rinsed it off and put it back into place. Believe it or not, that simple gesture started me on the right track and put me in the mood to at least brush my hair into a ponytail.

I wandered into the kitchen and started my Keurig. Coffee was just what I needed to push me through the morning. While I waited for it to brew, I picked up the remote to the small flat screen that was mounted in my kitchen and flipped through the channels. I stopped when I noticed a breaking story on Houston Sunshine, our local version of *Good Morning America*.

A Houston cop had shot a sixteen-year-old boy at Hermann Park last night. The teen died around four this morning. Of course he was black. I wanted to change the channel because I was fed up with these kinds of stories. This shit was getting out of hand and it was hard to watch, but something inside compelled me to continue listening. There were many unanswered questions surrounding the incident that led the officer to murder that kid, but I smelled a cover up coming.

Further complicating this story was that a black man, Jerome Powell, who was now being labeled a thug all over the media had been apprehended for allegedly getting some vigilante justice by shooting and fatally wounding the cop. For some reason I didn't feel sorry for the officer. I sympathized with the families of the teenage boy and Jerome. I'm not saying Jerome was justified in killing the cop, because murder is wrong in every sense of the word. But names like Michael Brown, Tamir Rice, Sandra Bland, and Eric Garner rang in my head. Not only them but I knew there were countless others who had been unjustifiably killed by the police and nothing had been done about it. In most cases, all of the officers involved had had prior complaints of racism. So at least this member of the legal police gang wouldn't be around to harm anyone else.

I mentally scolded myself for taking Jerome's side without knowing all the facts, then continued watching the news. A twenty-three-year-old man had fatally killed his own son over a potty training accident, two men had been killed in a car-jacking, a woman was kidnapped in broad daylight, flood warnings, earthquakes, and all of this had happened right here in Houston in just one day. I couldn't take any more so I flipped the television off, then pulled my coffee mug from the Keurig and took a sip. It was lukewarm, so I put it in the microwave to nuke it some.

The news broadcast had killed my vibe, so I walked into the living room, kicked off my house shoes, and plopped down on the sofa. I glanced at the wall clock. It was only 7:30 and I was already bored. You know what they say: an idle mind is the devil's workshop.

Corey once again took over my thoughts. I picked up my cell and flicked through my photo gallery at pictures of me and Corey. Pictures that he took reluctantly while at the same time making me promise to never post them on social media. He claimed it was because men don't put their business on the internet. But I knew it was really because he didn't want Felicia to know about us.

Instantly, I thought about making Facebook, Twitter, and Instagram accounts all dedicated to me and Corey. I tossed that thought quickly. That was too simple. It was an average chick's revenge and smooth talking ass Corey could find his way out of that shit. I needed something that was going to sit him down permanently.

Not sure of my next move, I paced around the living room trying to think of a master plan. I wasn't going to hurt Corey...

I was going to destroy him.

I walked and walked for what seemed like hours, but I just couldn't come up with anything. I looked out the window a few times just to pass the time. Then I tried to call Corey. When he didn't answer, something inside told me to go the place he shared with Felicia. If she had even an ant's brain, she should have left him by now, but in the event she hadn't I was going to pay her a visit.

I tidied up my ponytail and threw on the first thing I could find. A purple t-shirt with black accents, some cut up jeans, and a pair of black sandals. That would have to do. I grabbed my purse and rushed out the door. I knew exactly where they lived because I'd had to drop Corey off a few times in the middle of the night. I slid into the driver's side of my car and slung my purse into the passenger seat. A few loose pieces of paper flew out and onto the floorboard. I twirled my body around in the most awkward positions trying to gather every piece without having to get out of the car and walk around to the other side. Then I took off.

Once I got to Felicia's neighborhood, I made a few blocks just to get my mind right. Going to see the main chick started to seem as amateurish as making a Facebook page. That shit had been done before. I wanted something different. I parked down the street away from her place to gather my thoughts. Out the corner of my eyes, I caught a glimpse of something on the floor. I looked down and it was a piece of paper that I must have missed when I put everything back into my purse. It looked like a business card. I picked it up and checked it out.

Detective Davenport.

My eyes lit up. I finally knew what I was going to do. A few days ago, a couple of detectives were snooping around my place asking questions about Corey. But I have a disdain for the police, so I didn't give them the time of day. The most I could make out of what they were saying is that they felt like Corey was involved in an incident that left two men dead.

I grabbed my cell phone and dialed Corey. I called him five times and each of my calls were rejected. I shook my head and tried again. Same result. Well, Corey can't say I didn't give him a chance.

Next, I dialed the number on the card.

"Detective Davenport speaking."

"Hi, Detective. This is Gina Richards. You showed up at my

house the other day asking about Corey Wright."

"Yes. Yes. Ms. Richards, how are you?" I could hear a hint of excitement in his voice. It was if he knew I was about to give him something.

"I'm fine, sir. Listen, I wanted to know if you have a minute to meet with me. There are some things I'd like to talk to you about, but I don't want to come down to the station."

"Well. I was about to make a quick stop for a sandwich at Southern's. Can you be there in, say... fifteen minutes."

"Ironically, I'm down the street. I will be there in five." There was only one Southern's in all of Houston. It was more like a mom and pop shop, so I knew I had the right place.

"Okay. See you then."

I took a deep breath and called Corey once more.

"Come onnnnn Corey. Answer. Please answer. I don't want to do this to you."

When he didn't pick up, I decided I would go through with my plan. I didn't know anything about Joe-Joe's murder but that wouldn't stop me from telling the detective that Corey had confessed to me. I could gather enough information about the crime to make up a story with a quick Google search.

My hands trembled on the steering wheel. A wave of nausea hit me.

I opened the car door and released the butterflies that were floating around in my stomach, then I screeched out of the parking lot toward the sandwich shop.

Corey

I couldn't get into my hotel room fast enough. Yvette was all I could think about. I needed to find out what was going on. I couldn't talk to her until my head was right. I gutted me a White Owl and filled it with some Purp and smoked it like it was the last one on earth. After I was done, I felt like I could handle whatever Yvette was about to spring on me. I sat at the edge of the bed, picked up my cell, and dialed her number. It rang once. Yvette answered the phone on the first ring.

"What the fuck took you so long to call me back?" She yelled.

I didn't take the time to respond to her question. I wanted to know what she was saying when my phone cut us off.

"Naw. How about you tell me what you felt the need to do if I hadn't called you back?" I asked.

She breathed a long sigh. I could hear it resonate through the phone. Then, I heard tears and sniffles.

"I'm sorry Corey. The police had me stressed. They made Grammy get down on the floor like she was some common criminal," she screamed. "They had no regard for our well-being when they burst into her house."

I hated to hear her cry, but I needed to know that she had no plans to rat me out. "Look. All that is unfortunate. You know how the police are. That's why no matter what, you don't let them get to you. They are going to use this situation with your brother to get at me. You have to be strong." I tried to comfort her somewhat.

"All you care about is yourself. That's the only thing you can say to me? Well, how about we get down to it. You want to know if I would turn you in for my brother, right?" She questioned.

"Yeah. I do," I said straight up.

Yvette snapped.

"When were you going to tell me about the bitch who was going to have your baby? Here I am thinking I only was competing against Felicia. But I have to find out that you're having a baby and she lost it all in the same day!" She screamed louder. "It's too much! That's why I should make a deal to get my brother out. At least I know my brother will never lie to me…"

She paused. I remained silent. I didn't want to say anything to piss her off further.

"…but I'm not. Where are you? We need to talk." She said.

I breathed a sigh of relief. "Meet me at the hotel I took you to the first time we made love," I said.

Gina

I walked into the police station nervous as hell. I couldn't believe what I was about to do, but I did know it had to be done. I readjusted my clothes and checked myself out in the glass doors of the police station entrance before walking into the building. This meeting was supposed to have taken place at Southern's, but on the way to the restaurant, I got cold feet and backed out. Truth be told, I loved Corey and I didn't want to hurt him. But when I got home and thought about all he had put me through, I knew this had to be done.

I approached the desk where there was a female officer talking on the phone. "I will be right with you ma'am," she said pointing her finger at a sign-in sheet on the desk.

I signed my name and waited patiently for her to get off the phone. While waiting, I continued to scan the room. I don't know if I was looking for a sign that would send me running back out of the door or not. If there was a sign, it never presented itself.

"I apologize. How may I help you?" The officer asked.

I looked at her and my words would not come out. I drew a blank. "Ummm. I have an appointment with Detective---" I couldn't remember his name to save my life. "I'm sorry. Let me get the card out of my purse."

While I was searching for the detective's card, I guess the officer became agitated because I was taking too long. "Listen. Just give me your name. I will check while you continue to look."

"Gina Richards," I replied. "Never mind. I found it. His name is Detective Davenport."

She picked up the phone and advised Detective Davenport that his appointment was waiting in the lobby. "You can have a seat," she said pointing to a line of chairs in the waiting area.

I had another opportunity to change my mind. My mind was in conflict with my heart. I knew what I was about to do was wrong, but he had to pay. I refused to be used and abused. I am better than a side chick. I deserve to be the main chick.

"Hello Ms. Richards. Thank you for coming in. You can follow me," he said as he led the way.

"No problem detective. I apologize that I couldn't make it to the sandwich shop. Something came up suddenly."

The detective didn't give me much of a response. He just kept walking down a long hall. I knew it was real when he escorted me into a room with the word, INTERROGATION, written on the door. "Have a seat."

I sat down and he sat in a chair across from me. I guess he could tell I was nervous because he asked if I wanted something.

"If you have water, that would be great," I replied.

He left the room for what seemed like hours. When the door

opened, it wasn't Davenport. "Ms. Richards. My name is Detective Luis. Detective Davenport was called away to deal with another issue."

He pulled out a notebook and a pen. "Tell me what you know," he demanded as he glared at me with a stone face.

"What happened to my water?" I inquired as I cleared my throat.

He looked around and snidely replied, "I don't know anything about any water and my time is valuable. You called my partner and said you had information for us. This is a homicide and time is of the essence. So, lady, if you have something to tell us, then let me hear it."

He started to make me angry. He was treating me like I was the criminal. "I don't want to talk to you. I want to talk to Detective Davenport. Can you go get him? Don't forget to remind him to bring my water," I said with an air of confidence.

Corey

I didn't know what to think as I drove to the hotel room to meet Yvette. I couldn't believe she threatened me with turning me in to help her brother. I pulled into the parking lot and found a space that was away from the main entrance. I texted Yvette to let her know I was here.

She replied--Come to room 202. I jumped out of the car after looking around to make sure I wasn't being followed or about to get ambushed. When I felt comfortable, I walked up to the hotel room and knocked on the door. It took Yvette a few seconds to answer, but when she did--Damn! All the anger I had inside of me just melted away as I flashed back to the first time we made love at this hotel. I felt like a little bitch. I didn't have time for feelings. I needed to know where her head was at.

"What took you so long to answer the door? You had a nigga a little stressed standing out here waiting like that," I said as I pushed open the door. I tried to play hard as she attempted to give me a hug. I hoped she couldn't see through me. If she did, she would see how I wanted to rip her clothes off, throw her face down on the bed, and fuck the shit out of her from the back. But fucking was the last thing that should have been on my mind. I came here to find out what the hell she had been saying to the police.

Yvette

I walked to the mirror and double checked my reflection after I texted Corey and told him what room I was in. I was nervous as hell. I knew he was pissed at me for threatening him but I had some news for him that would rock his world. I decided that I would forgive Corey for that shit that went down with Brandi. From what the streets were saying, Brandi was a slut bucket and there was a high likelihood that her bastard baby didn't belong to my man anyway. Honestly though, that shit is in the past, her baby is dead. Time for us to all move on.

I pressed my lips together then blew a kiss to myself in the mirror just as I heard a light tap on the door. I ran my hand down my shirt to smooth out any wrinkles, took a deep breath and opened the door. As Corey walked in, I couldn't help but notice how sexy he was. I tried to grab him for a hug before he had a chance to fully close the door, but he was trying to act all hard and stuff. I hugged him anyway.

He smiled a little, then kissed my forehead, "That's not the greeting I was expecting. From the way you were threatening me earlier, I thought this was going to be a hostile meeting."

I didn't respond with words. Before I gave Corey the good news, my body wanted a different kind of attention. There was no way in the world, we'd meet up at the first hotel we'd ever made love in and not get it poppin'. I was soaking wet and ready. Without warning, I removed my shirt and leaned my body into his. I directed him over to the desk chair and told him to sit down. Corey looked surprised and hesitated a little.

"Yvette. Baby. So much is happening right now. I can't think about sex. I mean, I love you and I want you. It's just that…."

I didn't let him finish his sentence. I could see in his eyes that he wanted me too, so whatever he planned to say was bullshit. I needed some sexual healing and he was going to give it to me. I grabbed both of his hands and looked deeply into his eyes. Then I asked him nicely, yet seductively to sit down in the chair.

He complied.

I straddled and faced him. Then I pressed my lips against his and slid my tongue into his mouth. Slowly, but surely he loosened up and kissed me back. I knew I had him when I could feel his chest heaving in and out.

"Don't start no shit you can't finish," he said with a sexy smirk. He wrapped his arms around me, then stood me up and unbuttoned my pants. His hand traveled downward to my forbidden fruit. I closed my eyes and arched my back, inviting his touch. He kissed my neck as his finger made its way to my spot.

"Damn girl. Is all that wetness for me?" He didn't allow me to answer before he slowly and methodically walked us backward toward the bed.

Sparks flew and fireworks exploded as our bodies collided on the road to pure ecstasy. He took me to my peak three times. And I gave him the same in return.

Without saying a word, I went to the bathroom and started the shower. When I looked out into the room, Corey was sprawled across the bed half passed out.

I walked over and nudged him. "I see you're sweating like a horse. Wonder what that's from?" I asked playfully.

"All that work I just put in girl!" He responded.

"Shower time babe. I have something to tell you."

I stood behind Corey in the shower and washed him. I did that to show him that I had his back and always would. I rubbed a soapy sponge in circular motions from his shoulders down to his firm butt.

"That feels perfect, baby," he moaned.

"Thank you for coming Corey. I know you must have a lot on your plate. I just want you to know that I have your back. I know everything that I need to know about the shooting. I don't want you to give me any more details…."

"Good! Because I'm not talking about that shit, Yvette!" His mood shifted fast. His body tensed. I could tell things were turning sour.

"Hold on Corey. Listen to me. I think you will like what I have to say. I might have a way out of this for you. If that bitch Brandi can just keep her trap closed, I can save you both."

"I'm listening," he said. He turned around in the shower to face me. His eyes were deadlocked on mine.

"My brother…" My voice cracked a little. This was going to be hard for me to talk about, but Corey had to know.

I moved a little closer to my man and wrapped my arms around him as satisfyingly hot beads of water beat down over the both of us. Corey welcomed my hug and wrapped his arms around me as well. That gave me comfort.

The tears came from nowhere. I sniffled a little then continued to talk. "My brother is never getting out Corey. Do you remember the incident that was all over the news not long ago? A cop killed a teenager, then a black man killed the cop."

Corey nodded.

"Well, the killer is my brother. He pled guilty to it without a trial. You know the state of Texas is a death penalty state and they believe strongly in it. The DA offered my brother life in prison to plead guilty and my brother accepted to avoid the death penalty."

I dropped to my knees and cried. Corey turned off the water and stepped out of the shower, then he picked me up and out of the tub. He dried me off and wrapped a robe around me to warm me up because I was shivering cold. Then he found a robe for himself and carried me to the bed. All the while, he gently stroked my back to comfort me.

"I don't know what to say. I'm here for you. I love you, girl. I will do whatever I can to help you and your brother through this as long as I am out here on these streets." He used his thumb to wipe the tears that were still trickling down my face. "You know it's hectic out here for ya boy, though. I still have this case with Joe-Joe looming over my head."

"That's why I brought you here, Corey. I talked to my brother. He's willing to take the rap on that Joe-Joe shit, if we just take care of him while he is in there."

"Huh?!" Corey sounded shocked, but I could see the excitement all in his eyes. "What do you mean?"

"I mean, my brother is going to say that he set up the meeting with Joe-Joe and Mannie not knowing that they had bad blood. He is going to tell the police that it was a drug deal gone bad and that once Joe-Joe was dead, he killed Mannie to avenge his death.

Corey's eyes narrowed. He was happy, but I think he was skeptical. "How do I know I can trust your brother," he asked.

"You don't know that. But you trust me, right?"

He nodded.

"Ok then. I trust my brother and that's all the proof you should need.

Finally, his eyes lit up and his smiled widened. That was more of the reaction I was looking for. But what happened next was a complete shock.

Corey

"Damn girl, I love yo' ass!"

I didn't intend to do what I did. It just came out of nowhere. I was ecstatic. Yvette had a plan that could keep me out on these streets. It showed me that she was my real ride or die and before I knew it, I was down on one knee.

"Baby, will you marry me?"

She didn't move. I don't think what I was asking really hit her, so I said it again.

"I'm on bended knee. You are the only woman in this world for me. Marry me, please?"

She didn't speak, but the tears spilling from her eyes and her hand covering her mouth told me that I would probably be the groom in a wedding soon. I removed the diamond encrusted ring that I always wore on my pinky and slid it on her finger. Just as I did that, her head slowly began to nod, then finally came the words I was looking for.

"Yes, Corey. I will marry you!" She stood on her tiptoes and wrapped her arms around my neck before planting kisses all over my face.

When the moment of excitement passed, I stiffened just a tad. I stared off into space with my eyes bugged, looking like a deer caught in headlights. Did I really just do that?

Brandi

A few days had passed since my meeting with the detectives and I was still a nervous wreck. Thank God my sister had my back and brought her fine ass lawyer boyfriend in to defend me or I'm sure I'd be locked up right about now. The detectives were riding me hard and I was stumped but thanks to Carmelo, I made it through.

After our meeting, he advised me not to talk to anyone about the case. He told me all I had to do was keep my lips zipped and he was sure that he could get me off. He also warned me that at this point, I couldn't worry about what happened to Corey. Trying to play "captain save a Corey" could get me fucked off and land me a place in the joint sharing a cell with some big bitch named Precious who breathed hard and wanted my goodies.

With a sigh, I picked up my phone and start flipping through the photo gallery. My heart skipped a beat as I flicked through picture after picture of me with my baby bump. Tears began to fall. It was amazing to me how much I had come to love the little human that was growing inside of me. I'd never laid eyes on him a day in my life, yet I loved him more than I had ever loved anyone in my entirety. Getting past the loss of my son was going to take a ton of time.

I made my way into the nursery that Corey and I had painted and set up for the baby. I grabbed one of the receiving blankets and sprinkled a faint dusting of baby powder over it before I sat down in the rocker and held the blanket to my nose. More tears came and my breathing increased. I sat solemnly rocking back and forth. As the time passed I grew angry. How could Corey go on with his life as if our baby never existed? How would he justify not being there for me through this? What could he say or do to make this better. I racked my brain and there was nothing. I officially hated Corey. I wanted him to go to jail. I wished there was a way I could make him take the fall without being charged with a crime myself. I wanted to call those detectives and tell them everything, but I knew that would be self-incriminating and I wasn't prepared to go to prison.

Just as my thoughts started to get the best of me, I felt my phone vibrate in my hands. I looked down and it was Corey. I wanted to answer, but I wasn't ready to talk. As the phone rang, I anxiously tried to decide if I should pick up. Before I could make up my mind on what to do, the phone went dim and the vibrating stopped. I drew in a deep breath, then exhaled. Just as relief washed over me, the phone buzzed again. This time I answered without hesitation. At the least, I wanted to hear what he had to say.

"Hello."

"Hey Brandi! What's good girl?"

What the fuck did he mean by "what's good". Nothing was good. I had helped him set up Mannie which resulted in two people dying, I'd been shot and lost my baby, and I was part of a murder investigation. All of this was his fault and he hadn't called once to check on me or the baby. For all I knew, Corey wasn't even aware that I was no longer pregnant. I wanted to spaz out on him. But I didn't. I was done with Corey and he would never see me rattled.

So instead I answered plainly, "What's up, Corey?"

"Listen Brandi. We need to talk."

"Ok. So talk."

"I know a lot has happened lately and you must really hate me right now. But please understand that I always have and always will have your best interest at heart. I'm devastated by everything, but nothing crushed my soul like finding out that my son is dead. Trust me. It's killing me. I have to see you. There's some other shit you need to know. It's vital for us both. It won't make everything better, but it will be worth you hearing me out."

I didn't respond right away. One by one, memories of the night that changed everything flooded my brain. The "date" with Mannie, seeing Joe-Joe through the peephole, feeling the heat of a bullet penetrating my stomach, my stay in the hospital. Everything, and I do mean everything came back to me in that moment. Tears started to fall. A lump formed in my throat. The nerve of this man to call me with his fake ass concern. How dare he speak to me as if he has been hurt by this, yet never once had he called to check on me. He knew I had lost our son and he waited this long to reach out to me. I wanted to give him a piece of my mind. I needed to get it all out. Instead, I again reminded myself that he wasn't deserving of any emotion from me.

"Brandi? You still there?"

"I'm here Corey. We can talk whenever you want." That's all I said. I wasn't going to give him any more than that dry ass sentence.

"Ok. I will text you soon."

I disconnected without responding. When the call with Corey ended, I needed some wine and weed in the worst way. My anxiety level was through the roof. It took everything I had not to let loose on him. I poured myself a glass of wine and rolled a blunt. The moment I took the first sip, I could feel the nervousness exit my body. I lay back on my sofa and let the euphoria pass through me and after finishing the whole bottle, I passed out cold.

Gina

I sat in that interrogation room for over an hour before Detective Davenport returned. I wasn't sure why they were treating me like I was the criminal in this case. I was simply trying to help. As I waited in that scary room, I nibbled on my lower lip trying to think. The amount of time that had passed was making me regret the decision to take Corey down for some shit that I wasn't sure about at all.

I decided it was time for me to leave. Shaking with nervousness, I walked to the door, turned the knob, then eased it open and slowly walked down the hall. I wasn't sure why I was scared to walk out. Nothing said I was obligated to stay and speak with the detectives. I wasn't part of the crime. I hadn't been forced to come to the station. Everything I'd done was voluntary, so leaving was an option. Just as I made my exit from the room down the long hallway, Detective Davenport arrived holding a bottle of water in one hand and a file folder in the other.

"Going somewhere?" He asked.

I looked up at him. He definitely had a commanding presence. There was a hardness about him that I hadn't noticed earlier. I was intimidated to say the least. I rubbed my temple and then cleared my throat before speaking.

"Ummm. I got tired of waiting. I was in that room for over an hour. Besides, I'm not sure how much I can help with your investigation. I've had time to think about it and I believe I may have been over analyzing things. I'm sorry to have wasted your time, sir."

Detective Davenport extended his arm toward me to hand me the bottle of water. Then he swept past me back toward the interview room.

"Follow me," he said without looking back.

I sat in silence across the table from him. I didn't want to be back in that room. I no longer wanted to hurt Corey, but I was already there. I'd already promised the detective that I had some information that could help his case.

"Tell me what you know."

I pressed my lips together tightly. Clenched my jaws. The truth was that I didn't know anything, but Detective Davenport wasn't letting me off the hook. He slid his seat close to mine and placed the folder he'd been holding in the hallway onto the table, then he spread the contents in front of us both. He sat up straight in his chair, propped his elbows on the table and stared me down.

"Both of these men are dead, Gina," he said, pointing to the pictures of Joe-Joe's and Mannie's lifeless bodies.

I closed my eyes. I wasn't prepared to see those pictures. This shit was getting too real for me. I couldn't take any more. Tears started to pour from my eyes. I'm sure the detective saw that as me breaking down to give him some vital information, but in all actuality it was the guilt I'd began to feel about doing this to Corey.

"Don't commit a crime by becoming an accessory after the fact, Ms. Richards. If you have information that can help us solve this case, it would be in your best interest to tell us what you know."

I took a sip of my water, then pushed my chair away from the table. I rubbed both of my hands up and down my face in a fit of apprehension. Without thinking, my lips parted and out came the words, "Ok. I'll tell you everything I know."

Yvette

It was a little after noon the day after Corey proposed. I walked across the tattered and creaking boards of Grammy's front porch into her shabby living room. She was sitting in her favorite recliner, shelling peas with a pair of metal rimmed glasses on the edge of her nose.

"Hey Grammy," I said making my way over to give her a hug.

She looked up at me and smiled. "Good to see you baby."

And even though Grammy smiled, her eyes told me that she wasn't happy. She looked tired and run down. Dark circles surrounded her bloodshot eyes. Without any words from Grammy, I knew that what had happened to my brother was taking its toll on her.

"I'm getting married, Grammy!" I said waving my hand in her face. I didn't officially have an engagement ring, but I was still wearing Corey's diamond pinky ring.

She dropped more peas into the bowl on her lap and tossed the hull into a garbage bag on the floor. Then she crossed her arms and gave me the side eye. "Married, huh? Umph!"

I was stunned by her reaction. I didn't expect her to jump and dance a jig, but I did expect her to smile and offer her congratulations. I thought such good news would help her forget about Jerome for a minute. Instead it seemed to piss her off.

"I hope you don't expect me to come to the wedding. I ain't celebrating shit. My baby is gone Yvette! You hear me? My baby's gone. He ain't ever getting out and you waltz in here with that ring on your finger talking about getting married! How can you be happy, huh? How could you be so selfish? Your brother gone die in prison and I'm gone die of a broken heart!"

For the first time since Corey had proposed, my smile faded. I hated to see Grammy so upset. I knew she was hurting about what happened to Jerome. We all were hurt. But I still thought she would be happy for me. Sitting around sulking wasn't going to bring him home. He killed a police officer and even though it was vigilante justice, in the United States of good ole America, he had committed a crime that was punishable by death. In my opinion, we should have been happy that the state of Texas wasn't going to put a needle in his arm.

I wanted to reach out and console Grammy, but I was scared to death. She had a reputation for being crazy. I backed away from her and made my way to the door to let myself out. Before I could turn the knob, Grammy abruptly got up from the chair and charged past me.

"Get yo' ass on out my house, gal! I'm not for the foolishness today. I just ain't! So gone, now. Go!"

I was upset about the way Grammy was treating me, but I knew she still loved me. I knew that deep inside her anger stemmed from hurt. I didn't leave. Instead, I walked over to where she was standing and slid my arms around her neck.

"I love you Grammy. I'm sorry that I was insensitive about Jerome. He's my brother and I love him. I'm hurting too. But I went to see him and he was in good spirits. My comfort came from that visit. You should go see him. You will feel better."

Grammy embraced me, then broke down into tears. I'd never seen her so distraught and it was killing me. I held her tight because she needed me.

"Get it all out, Grammy. Get it out."

Corey

It had been a long week. I took a drag from my blunt as I navigated my ride onto the street toward the apartment I had got for me and Yvette. Neither of us had been staying there since all the bullshit with Mannie and Joe-Joe had popped off, but I was tired of living at the hotel so I decided I was going home.

I was in a good mood. I had just met up with Brandi and explained to her that I had a way out of this situation for us. It was a hard being around her at first because she was so distressed over losing our son that it killed me to see her like that. Once we moved past that conversation, I told her that I needed her to trust me. I didn't want to come out and tell her that Yvette's brother was going to take the fall for us. I simply told her that I had a plan that would keep us both out of prison and the only way it would work is if she would just be quiet.

She let me know that her sister had hired Carmelo Montiago and he'd instructed her keep her mouth closed as well, so I wasn't too worried about her speaking out anymore because if she knew anything about Carmelo, she would know that he's the best and she'd do everything he told her to do. I knew of the cat and he was dope as hell. He helped one of my homeboys get off on some shit he'd been caught on camera doing, so I knew Carmelo was the truth. I used it to my advantage and told her she should do everything he instructed. That's when she told me that she wasn't supposed to have any dealings with me until after everything had blown over. We parted ways and I told her I'd be in touch. That's when I decided to finally go home.

I nearly choked when I pulled up in front of the apartment. A black on black SUV sitting in my parking lot could only mean one thing. I smashed the blunt out in the ashtray and instead of parking decided to bust a U-turn. I knew it wouldn't be long before the detectives who'd been harassing all of my friends would come looking for me. And even though I had a plan, I was in no mood to deal with them.

When I turned the car around, I got the shock of my life. Three police cars pulled up on me from all different directions, out of nowhere. At the same time, the detectives pulled behind me in their unmarked SUV. I was surrounded. There was nowhere to go. Before I knew what happened, they were all getting out of their vehicles, guns drawn and yelling at me.

One of the officers yelled through a bullhorn, "Get out of the car with your hands up, now!"

I froze.

"Now!" He yelled again.

I opened the door slowly and removed myself from my truck one leg at time. I thought about running, but all the guns pointed at my head convinced me otherwise. My heart and mind raced simultaneously as I thought about all the young, black men who'd been killed at the hands of police while surrendering. I said a silent prayer to God to keep me safe. Two of the cops rushed toward me as soon as both of my feet hit the ground.

"Turn around and put your hands behind your back."

I did as I was told and the cop handcuffed me.

"You have the right to remain silent…"

Yvette

"What do you mean, you're in jail, Corey?" I asked hysterically.

"I need you to listen to me, baby. They picked me up from the crib, but everything is going to be ok."

I sat straight up in the bed and let what he just said sink in. My chest tightened and my heart raced as my man described how the police had blocked him in at our apartment and took him down to the station. He gave me instructions to go meet his boy, Tony to pick up bail money and to come get him as soon as possible. My heart slowed down a little when I heard the word bail because I knew he was going to come home, but I still had a ton of questions.

"Oh my gosh, honey. What the hell is going on? Please, Corey, tell me something."

"I'll explain when you get here. Just do like I asked and hit Tony. Tell him they got me and he'll meet you with the dough. Then call my lawyer, Alexander Drake. Tell him you have the money and he will meet you down here to pick me up. My time's up. I have to go. Just hurry and get here. Love you."

"Love you, too."

I disconnected the call and jumped up out of the bed at Grammy's house. I rushed around the room, putting on clothes and shoes while at the same time I frantically dialed Tony's number.

"Tony!" I yelled into the phone the moment he answered.

"What up?" He asked calmly.

"They got Corey!" I screamed.

"What do you mean, they got Corey? Who is they?"

"The police. My man's in jail. He told me to call you and..."
He cut me off before I could finish, "Yvette, I need you to calm down. Head to my house. I'm not there, but I will call Keisha and tell her to give you everything you need. When you get to Corey and he's out, tell him I will be at the spot waiting."

***

I sat on the hard concrete stairs outside of the Harris County Courthouse waiting for Corey's attorney to arrive just as I had been instructed. My nerves were on edge with so many police swarming around the around the area. My mind kept going back to the day they busted down Grammy's door looking for my brother, Jerome. Believe it or not, I was still traumatized by that incident. Tears threatened to fill my eyes as I thought about Jerome, but I blinked them away. I told myself I had to be strong.

It was almost a hundred degrees out. The smoldering Texas heat was beginning to get a little uncomfortable. As sweat gushed from my pores, the skin tight romper short set I was wearing clung to my skin. I stood up to adjust my clothes, then I pulled a napkin from my purse and wiped my forehead as I looked around for Attorney Drake to arrive. I had been waiting for over an hour and there was still no sign of him.

"Where the hell is he?" I mumbled aloud, talking to myself.

I looked at my mobile phone just to be sure I didn't have any missed calls or texts. I wanted to call and lose it on him, but I decided that wouldn't be a good idea, since he was my man's only hope of freedom. It was crazy because I still didn't know exactly what Corey was locked up for, I could only hope it didn't have anything to do with the murders.

Just as my patience began to wear thin, I heard someone call out my name. I turned around expecting to see the lawyer. Instead, it was Shawn. My eyes bugged wide. Shawn was the last person I wanted to see. My heart thudded just a tad and I took a few steps back as Shawn moved closer to me.

"Shawn."

"Yvette."

I looked him square in the face, trying to hide the angst that was rushing through my veins. Shawn looked crazy. Something about his eyes told me that this was going to be bad. I tried to back up a little more but my body was frozen in fear. Before I could think or move, Shawn was standing directly in front of me. He looked all jacked up. His eyes were bloodshot red like he was high on something heavy.

I scanned the area, trying to make eye contact with one of the many police officers that I'd seen swarming earlier, but I didn't see not one cop at all. I looked back toward Shawn and he was staring at me. He stroked my face. The roughness of his hands surprised me because they were once so soft. He leaned toward me and whispered in my ear, "I miss you, Yvette."

His breath reeked of stale cigarettes and liquor. I wanted to scream for help, but I was too afraid. He rubbed his hands along my exposed thighs and continued talking to me as if things were normal between us. I was instantly nauseous.

"I've been going crazy without you baby. I need you. Please come back to me. Give me a chance to show you that I've changed. I'll take care of you. Please, baby. You deserve better than a nigga like that punk ass dude, Corey. Now that he's locked up, it can be just me and you."

A chill ran up my spine. "Huh? How did you find me here? Who told you about Corey and that he was in jail?"

"I have my ways Yvette. Don't you worry about that." He lowered his head and moved closer as if he was going to kiss me. Again, I froze. Stood there all stiff and rigid waiting for the contact of his big soup cooler ass lips against mine. But instead of kissing me, he put his face extremely close to mine and whispered in my ear again.

"Turn around," he said through gritted teeth. I felt something hard and cold pressed into my back as he spoke.

My stomach knotted up as I did as I was told. I couldn't believe things had shifted so quickly. One minute I was sitting outside the courthouse waiting to meet Corey's attorney, then in a split second, I was walking away from that very spot at gunpoint. There were so many people around, yet it seemed that nobody noticed what was happening with me and Shawn.

I moved slowly, praying for a miracle as I walked. Where the fuck was that punk ass lawyer? He should have been here by now. I felt my phone buzz in my purse. Maybe it was Mr. Drake. I wanted to answer, but I knew that would set Shawn off. Finally, we made it to a car. It was a blacked out Chevy Impala. The windows were tinted so dark, I couldn't see inside.

"Get in!" He said as he forcefully grabbed me by the arm and pushed me into the backseat of the car.

Corey

After I'd been locked up behind bars for hours, a slender built female guard with a long blond ponytail called my name.

"Corey Wright?"

I stood from the hard metal bench, faced her, and nodded.

"Your bond has been posted, and you're free to go."

I drew in a deep breath, then blew it out in relief. It was a wonderful feeling to know that my girl had done exactly as she was instructed and came through for me.

"Head this way." The guard smiled at me and gently touched my hand, as she escorted me from the cell block to the processing area.

I kind of laughed inwardly at her actions. The look in her eyes told me that I could have her if I wanted. But I didn't have it in me to try and get at her. I didn't need any new thots in my lineup, especially not a police bitch, considering all the trouble I was trying to get myself out of these days.

Once they gave me all of my paperwork and the information for when I had to return to court, I was told I was free to go. I counted the cash to make sure every dollar of the three grand I had on me when I was arrested was still there. Then I got my cell phone and all of my other belongings and walked out front expecting to see my lady and my lawyer, but the only face I saw was that of Mr. Drake.

"Sorry it took so long, I had an appointment that ran late and then I couldn't reach Yvette by phone," he said, shaking my hand.

The smile I'd been wearing faded. What the hell did he mean Yvette didn't answer the phone? I shook it off and thanked my attorney for coming. He advised me to call his office to schedule an appointment to talk about the case and we went separate ways. As soon as I made it outside, I started calling Yvette like crazy. She never answered and I was immediately pissed off. I rushed by foot from the jail down to the courthouse where Yvette was supposed to meet my lawyer. By the time I made it there, I saw my girl being forced into a car by that nigga Shawn.

Yvette

I couldn't believe that I was in the back of Shawn's damn car---kidnapped. What kind of shit had this nigga been smoking? My heart was beating so hard that the thumps seemed as though they were radiating out of my ears. I couldn't use my phone to call for help because the fool had my purse in the front seat with him. It seemed as though he'd been planning this for a minute. There was a plexiglass partition separating the front and back seats like a cab or limo. I thought about opening the door and jumping out at the stoplight, but when I tried, it was like the doors were sealed shut. The locks on the door had been fixed so that you couldn't open either door. I guessed he'd activated the child safety locks on the doors. The tint on the widows were so dark that I could see people looking right at me, but they could not see me or the panic that had engulfed my body. What was happening to me was surreal. I was the star in a real life *TV One* episode of *Fatal Attraction*.

"Shawn. I know you can hear me. Why in the hell are you doing this to me?" I screamed, banging on the plexiglass so hard that my knuckles started to sting and turn red.

"Shut up! Shut up! You're interrupting my song," he yelled back at me.

He turned the radio up louder and started singing, "I saw you and him...walking in the rain."

Shawn had truly lost his mind. "Let me go. Where are you taking me?"

He didn't respond, but he did turn up the music and sang louder and louder. It seemed like we had been driving for hours before he finally stopped. We were at a BP gas station, but I wasn't sure which one. As I scanned the area, it wasn't anywhere that I recognized. When I saw him walk into the store, I started to bang on the windows. I kicked and I screamed. I hoped that the people at the pumps would hear me, but they didn't. It seemed as though they were looking dead at me. If they did hear me, they weren't trying to get involved. Deep down inside, I didn't blame them. I probably wouldn't help either. Shit, I've seen what happens to the fools who try to be heros. They end up dead. I just hope that at least someone will write down the license plates number and call the damn cops. At least that would give me a fighting chance. I stopped banging and screaming when he returned to the car. He pumped the gas and hopped back in the car. This time, he opened the partition and threw me a Banana Nut Bread cake and a can of Coke. The can hit me in the forehead.

"Ouch! What the hell you do that for?" I screamed out in pain.

"Oh baby, I am so sorry. I didn't mean that," he apologized.

I saw a tenderness in his eyes that wasn't there at first, so I played on it.

"Why are you trying to hurt me Shawn? I thought you loved me. I love you," I lied.

"Liar!" he screamed. "You damn skank ass bitch. If you loved me, you wouldn't be fucking that criminal."

Shawn slammed the partition, locked it, and sped out of the parking lot. He'd pulled out of the gas station so violently it was like a dust storm had taken over the gas station with all the debris that flew everywhere. I decided that it may be in my best interest to just be still and observe my surroundings as much as possible. I was deep in thought as we rode down the highway. I couldn't believe he referred to Corey as a criminal. How could he possibly know anything about Corey? All of a sudden it came to me, Shawn called the police on Corey. It all made sense now. That's why he was at the police station. He knew I was going to be there to bail Corey out. That motherfucker! Had Shawn been following me? Did he have my phone tapped? Had he been stalking me? All of these question scrolled in my mind like credits from a movie.

I was broken out of my thoughts when the car came to sudden stop. I noticed that we were getting farther and farther away from the city and when we stopped in front of an old, Victorian style house, I knew exactly where we were. I had only been there one other time and that was when Shawn's grandmother died.

"Why did you bring me here," I screamed out. The tears began to flow. A feeling of pending death coveted my soul. My heart dropped into my stomach. I began to feel sick.

"Why did you bring me here!" I screamed again.

He snatched me out of the car by the arm. His grip was so tight it felt like his fingers were penetrating my skin and touching my bone. I cried out in pain.

"You're going to learn today that you can't play with a man's heart and that shit won't come back and haunt you," he said as he dragged me into the living room of the house.

The house smelled like old people, mothballs and mildew. He slammed me down onto a couch that was covered in white sheets. It was like an Amityville Horror movie. He pulled out some gray duct tape and wrapped my ankles together. He pushed me forward. My forehead hit my knees with such force, I felt the point of impact begin to swell. Shawn walked over to the big window and reached up to pull the shades down. His shirt lifted just far enough for me to see his Beretta. It was the same one that he taught me how to shoot. Shawn was a great marksman. I prayed that tonight I wasn't going to be used for target practice. I began to pray.

"Dear Lord. Bless him. He doesn't know what he is doing. The devil has his soul right now Lord. Please help him see that what he is doing or about to do goes against your will," I chanted out loud. I wanted him to hear me. "God, deliver me from this evil situation."

Shawn stopped in his tracks. He turned to me and said with a voice that I hardly recognized, "I know I had my flaws, but I loved you. All I wanted was for you to love me too. Love me-- my flaws and all. You had to go and get with some thug who got more women, more problems, and is just as flawed. Dumb bitch! God ain't go help you tonight. Tonight we end this foolishness--one way or the other."

Corey

Shit was crazy. My mind was on an emotional roller coaster ride. When I was finally released from jail, I was pissed that Yvette didn't come through for me, but once I got outside the courthouse where she was supposed to meet my attorney, I saw that nigga Shawn putting her in a blacked out Impala. I scanned the area for her vehicle, but quickly realized that even if I could find it, I didn't have a key. I raced toward them, but Shawn had her in the car and was pulling off before I could get close enough to whoop his ass and save my baby.

I looked up toward the sky and said a quick prayer to God to help me. Before I could finish my request a taxi pulled up out of nowhere, and it was just in the nick of time. I opened the back door and hopped in.

"Follow that black car. Here's two hundred dollars to get started. I don't give a damn how long they drive, don't you lose them and don't you stop 'til they stop!" I yelled.

The cab driver kind of hesitated, so I held up a wad of cash. "Just go! There's more where that came from and a big tip in it for you if you catch them!"

Gina

I waited in that back room as long as I could. I was itching to come out and reveal myself. The whole time I was back there all I could think about was how those damned detectives tried to get me all caught up. As a matter of fact, they almost fucked up the whole plan. If that persistent ass detective hadn't of come back so fast, I would have made it out the door. Shit, I really didn't want Corey to go to jail. I loved him. In jail, he would be do me no good. But I did want him to hurt so bad that he would eventually have no other choice but to come running back to me. Like a lioness in the pack, there could only be one Alpha female---that was me. So, I knew what I had to do. Instead of making up some lame ass lie about Joe-Joe's murder, I made a quick decision to go along with Shawn's plan to take Corey down.

Shawn and I bumped into each other on a chance encounter. We first met at Taj's Bar and Grill. We were both seated at the bar and struck up a conversation. He bought me a Long Island Iced Tea while he downed a couple of shots of Grey Goose. We were both lit. We started talking about how fucked up our relationships were. I told about Corey and all of his bullshit. He told me about Yvette and how she left him for some nigga named Corey. "How fucking ironic," I thought to myself. We talked more and found out we were moving in the same circles. Bam! Plan 'Get Your Boo Back' began for us both. This plan took up a lot of our time. We became stalkers. By the time we finished our surveillance, we could almost predict every move Corey and Yvette would make--before they did.

When Shawn first asked me to help him set Corey up, I was hesitant to go along with it, but I had to tell the detectives something because they had me trapped in that interrogation room. So when I said I'd tell them everything I knew, I spit out all the shit I'd discussed with Shawn. Next thing I knew, I was hiding in the back room of Shawn's grandmother's creepy old abandoned house waiting for him to deliver Yvette.

I just couldn't take it anymore. "Oh stop all of that motha fucking praying you ugly ass, bitch," I said as I walked out of the back bedroom. "I don't see what the fuck Corey ever saw in you. You a damn troll."

Yvette looked at me, but had no idea who I was. I knew her, though.

"Who the fuck are you?" she yelled. "Why in the hell are you here?"

She looked at Shawn. "Who is this woman Shawn? What is going on? I need to know why you are doing this," Yvette quizzed.

Shawn looked at me. I knew he was mad. He had not given me the signal to come out of the room. *Fuck his signal.*

"I didn't give you the signal. I told you not to come out until it was time," Shawn yelled.

"First of all, you don't tell me to do a damn thing. I'm not your bitch. Second of all, you were taking too long. I was getting impatient. Plus, I didn't want you out here getting all soft and shit. We got to follow the plan." I checked Shawn, letting him know that I ain't no timid ass bitch.

I walked up to Yvette and smacked her. "That's for fucking my man."

I knew she wanted to get at me, but her hands were tied. Smack. Smack. Smack. I continued to smack the sides of her face. I hated her with a passion.

"Stop!" Shawn yelled. "I never said you could put your hands on her. She belongs to me."

"I don't belong to no one," Yvette responded. "...Bitch, you better be glad this fool got me tied up because this troll would beat your ass."

My emotions got the best of me. I said, "Let me see you try it." I ripped the tape from around her wrists and ankles.

Shawn started yelling, "You crazy ass bitch! What are you doing?"

I squared up and said, "You bad. You were talking all that shit. What you going to do now?"

Yvette jumped to her feet and threw a punch that grazed the side of my face. I grabbed her by the shoulders and tried to knee her in the stomach. Shawn desperately tried to break us apart, but couldn't. All of the anger I had pinned up was released.

Pop! Pop! Pop!   Three shots went off. Yvette and I both were so startled by the gunfire, we stopped in our tracks. "What the fuck you doing?" I took my eyes off of Yvette and focused on crazy ass Shawn.

"Both of you, sit your asses down!" He screamed. His eyes were glazed over.

Next thing I knew, I was bound and gagged--right beside the troll.

Corey

I was nervous as hell the whole cab ride. For one, I didn't have a pistol on me and for two, I could only imagine how scared my girl must have been. I could tell the cab driver was hesitant to be involved because he kept looking at me through the rearview mirror and talking shit. When Shawn stopped at the BP gas station that would have been the best time for me to make a move on him, but I figured he had a gun so I decided to chill. All I could think about was what if something went wrong and I ended up dead. I couldn't be stupid and approach the nigga without a weapon. Plus, I had to think about Yvette, too I had to make sure she came out of this thing alive.

I sat in the back of the taxi and contemplated my next move. Damn! I needed a blunt and a miracle. It's like the good Lord was on my side because I spotted my boy Tony coming out of the store. The BP was close to the safe house where me and Tony conducted a lot of our business. Yvette told me Tony said he would be waiting at the house for me, so I wasn't too surprised to see him in the area at the gas station.

Shawn was still in the store when Tony walked out. I told the driver to pull to the side of the BP so I could keep my eyes on that Impala, but also so Shawn wouldn't spot me. Then I called Tony.

"My nigga! I see they finally let yo' ass up out the slammer," he said jokingly into the phone.

"Tony. I'm at the BP by the spot. Pull up on the side of the building, next to the Yellow Cab. I know you strapped up! That nigga Shawn done kidnapped my girl!"

The phone clicked off and the next thing I knew Tony pulled up beside us. I threw the driver another hundred dollars and hopped in the car with my boy just in time for us to pull out behind Shawn. Tony wanted details about what happened, but all I could tell him was how I got hemmed up at the apartment and hauled off to jail.

"... Then when Mr. Drake showed up without Yvette, I had a funny feeling in my stomach. I rushed over to the courthouse just in time to see that dude forcing her into his ride. The panicked look on her face told me everything I needed to know."

We rode in silence after I said that. Tony was a goon. I knew he was envisioning everything he planned to do to Shawn once we caught him. I think he got a little nervous when Shawn turned down a long, winding dirt road because he lifted the middle console in his car and pulled out a 9mm. Then he told me to open the glove box and get the .45. I swear we drove for about ten minutes down that road. I normally don't fear nothing but I can't lie, that shit had a brother shook. As we went farther down the road, I told Tony to fall back some. I didn't want Shawn to spot us behind him and do something stupid.

Finally, I could see an old, white house in the distance. My stomach dropped. I could tell the house was abandoned. The paint was chipped and one of the windows upstairs was boarded up. We watched from afar as Shawn forced Yvette out of the car and into the house. The moment he went inside and closed the door, Tony put his truck in park about 200 yards away. We jumped out and raced toward the house in a full sprint. Then we heard three pops.

Tony dropped to the ground. I kept running. My heart wouldn't let me stop. I had to get to Yvette. This is not how I wanted it to end. If this nigga killed my girl, I was going to make him regret every minute of the rest of his life. Once I made it to the house, I jumped from the ground straight onto the porch. I kicked the door in without giving it a second thought. Then I froze. I couldn't believe my eyes. Both Gina and Yvette were bound to chairs. And Shawn was pointing a gun at the door.

"Gina?! What the fu…"

Before I could finish my sentence, I felt a hard thud in my back and gunshots rang out. Tony had rushed in behind me and pushed me to the floor. The brightness of gunfire filled the room. Bullets were flying in every direction. But my boy Tony is a sharp shooter. When he dove into me and knocked me on the floor, he aimed his nine right for Shawn's head. Two shots and brain matter flew everywhere. Shawn's head exploded and his body hit the old creaky floor with a loud thump before he could react. Both of the girls screamed in high pitch squeals. Everything happened so fast.

I quickly ran over to Yvette and pulled the duct tape from her hands and feet. She jumped up, wrapped her arms around me and planted kisses all over my face as tears streamed down her face.

"I thought I was going to die. I love you! I love you! I love you, Corey!"

I leaned in and gave her all of my tongue. For a moment, we were the only people in the room. Fuck that. We were the only people in the world. But that only lasted a second.

"Ok, love birds. Get a room! Better yet, just stop that shit. We have a dead man on the floor and a crazy bitch tied to a chair. Now ain't the time for being lovey, dovey. We have to get the hell out of this house before it's surrounded by police and we all end up in jail," Tony said.

"Tony's right. Let's go," I said as I grabbed Yvette's hand to lead her out of the house.

Yvette stopped walking before we got to the door. "But what about her?" She asked, pointing to Gina.

"What about her? We're leaving her ass here. She will have to get back to the city on her own."

"But who is she?"

"Hell if I know." I lied.

I could tell Yvette knew better, but she had already been through so much, she didn't object. We followed Tony to his car and he drove us the opposite direction up the dirt road, back into the city.

Brandi

It had been months since the fiasco that claimed the lives of both Mannie and Joe-Joe had happened. My run-in with the law seemed so far behind me. After my brother-in-law slash attorney told me that any pending charges against me and Corey had been dropped because another man confessed to the crime, I didn't hear from Corey at all. I was puzzled for a long time as to how Corey convinced someone else to take the rap for a crime that I knew we committed together. But I decided very quickly that I wasn't going to worry too much about it.

Things were going okay until I heard that Corey was getting married in a couple of weeks. I was so depressed that I couldn't eat or sleep. Finding out that he had decided to wife another bitch so soon after we called it quits brought a flood of emotions back into my mind. I wondered if he had been creeping with her the whole time we were together.

I decided to investigate. I told myself if I found out that nigga had a side bitch while I was pregnant and doing his dirty work, I was going to DESTROY him. On top of all that, I couldn't shake the thoughts of the baby I lost. I was still sitting up late nights in the nursery, pushing that brand new rocking chair back and forth as I cuddled up to the same ole powder dusted blanket that I'd been sniffing since I came home from the hospital. Only now, I'd graduated from baby powder to a little cocaine to powder my nose and keep my mind right.

The fact that Corey was getting married had me bugging. I decided to get with my homegirl Jasmine. She was deep in the streets. She knew everyone and everyone's business so I called her up and invited her over to get on some of that fluffy white stuff with me. She always willingly gave me the tea when I got her high.

Yvette

My cousin Jasmine called to let me know that Brandi had been sniffing around asking questions about me. Well, actually, Brandi was trying to get some dirt on "Corey and the bitch he was marrying". I laughed it off and told Jasmine that I didn't give a damn.

"She wants to know about the 'bitch he's marrying', huh? Why the hell does she care? I thought I got rid of her when you helped me make that fake Facebook page. Girl, please! I'm planning a wedding. Life couldn't be better. I don't have time for that mess."

"What if he's still fucking her, though?" Jasmine asked, being her usually messy self.

"Come on cousin. Do you really believe that? If he was still with Brandi we would both know. But anyway, what do you think about this dress for my bridesmaids?" I asked, holding up my iPad so she could see the picture of the dress on the bridal website I was browsing.

"Ok! I see you cuz." Jasmine exclaimed.

"You really like it?" I asked a little perplexed as to why she was making such a big deal about a dress I hadn't even made a decision to buy.

"Oh, yea. The dress. I like it. But honestly, I'm talking about that two carat diamond you're rocking. When did you get that?"

"Corey surprised me with it a few days ago," I said laying the iPad on the coffee table and holding my left hand up so Jasmine could get a better view of my rock. Low-key I was glad she noticed it. I kind of wanted her to be jealous. It wasn't to be mean, it was just that all my life, I'd been the ugly chick. When we were in high school, all of the guys wanted to get with Jasmine. Any boy that I liked, liked her. And she didn't care. She dated two different guys that I had crushed on. I confronted her both times and each time she jokingly said, "Girl, I can't help don't nobody want yo' ugly ass." That was hard on the soul.

Now, I was marrying the love of my life, one of the best catches in the city of Houston, and Jasmine was the single mother of three children with three different fathers.

Corey

"Dude, you shaking like a damn leaf on a tree. Calm down," Tony said. "You act like I am taking you to the last supper or something."

"I promised Yvette that there would be no strippers at the bachelor party," Corey said, shaking his head at Tony. "I know you got something up your sleeve."

We finally pulled up to our destination. It was the Four Seasons.

As we walked in, I began to reminisce about my homie, Joe-Joe. Tony is my boy. He a ride or die nigga, but Joe-Joe was my cousin, more like my brother. I missed him. The truth is, I still felt some guilt. It's my fault he's not here and I got to live with that shit. It felt even worse knowing that I didn't attend his funeral, but I couldn't take any chances.

"Smells like Eucalyptus plants up in this bitch," Tony said looking around trying to find the source.

"That's how you know we in a five-star hotel fool. Otherwise, we would be smelling smoke and mildew," I laughed nervously. I still wasn't sure what Tony had planned, but I damn sure wasn't going to do anything to jeopardize my pending marriage. Yvette would kill my ass.

We rode the elevator up to Floor 20, the Presidential Suite. Tony took the key card and when we walked in I couldn't believe my eyes.

Our entire crew stood there with bottles ready to pop.

"It's your bachelor party fool," yelled Ramon, one of my top dogs. He ran my trap house on the Northside of town.

I couldn't believe how my boys came out and showed all this love. I really wished my cousin and homie, Joe-Joe, was here to see this shit. I let my guard down, pulled my stash out of my bag, and rolled me a nice old blunt. As a matter of fact, there were so many blunts being passed around the room, I was so fucked up that I thought I was seeing Joe-Joe. "This some good ass weed. This shit got me thinking I see Joe-Joe" I said to Tony as I passed him another one.

"Nigga, you ain't that damn high. That is Joe-Joe!" Tony screamed like a bitch. "When the hell dead people come to motha fucking bachelor parties?"

The entire room got quiet. Niggas who were standing up sat down and niggas sitting down stood to their feet in disbelief. Some of the scary ass dudes left the room. I took a mental note of all the weak links in my circle.

"What's up bro?" Joe-Joe said as he walked towards me with his arms stretched out wide.

I didn't know whether to shoot him or embrace him.

"You know I wouldn't miss this night for the world," Joe-Joe said. "Witness protection couldn't keep me away from being here to celebrate your special day. You do remember that if it wasn't for me, you and Yvette would have never gotten together in the first place."

"I remember, but don't tell nobody else that shit. I might have to kill you--again," I laughed and grabbed my boy and we went into the back room. People were still looking like they had seen a ghost. I knew it wasn't a ghost because I could feel him. It was Joe-Joe. I wanted to burst into tears, but I wasn't going out like no damn punk.

"It's not like I ain't glad to see you, but all this time I have been thinking you were dead. As a matter of fact, they had a funeral in your name nigga. You got some explaining to do," I demanded. "Did I hear you say something about a witness protection?"

Joe-Joe looked at me and like the man of so little words he was, he said, "God just wasn't ready for a nigga like me to go yet."

Gina

"I wonder if you can really die of a broken heart," I thought to myself when Corey walked out the door with that bitch Yvette and left with no regard for me.

If a broken heart could kill, I would have died on the spot. Honestly, I didn't see life worth living anymore. Nobody meant more to me than Corey had. I gave him all of me. Everything I lived and breathed for had to do with making him happy. Maybe I should have been honest from the start. I shouldn't have tried that reverse psychology bullshit that had worked for Tracy.

I sat in that old rickety chair with my hands bound for hours. I could've freed myself long ago. I'd seen an episode of *20/20* a few months back where they had an ex FBI agent talk about safety. I listened intently as he described how to break free if you ever found yourself bound by duct tape. I didn't think I'd ever have to use it, yet here I was with my hands and feet tied together and a dead body less than ten feet away.

I stared at Shawn. His head had been blown to smithereens. I wanted to cry, but I was too numb. Honestly I didn't feel sorry for him. He deserved what he got, but so did I.

I spent twenty-four entire hours looking at Shawn's lifeless body before I made a decision of my own. The Beretta he'd fired to stop me and Yvette from arguing was still clutched in his hands. Corey's friend came in shooting so fast, Shawn had no time to react. I stared at the gun. Wondered if anyone would miss me when I was gone. Decided they wouldn't. And even if someone did miss me, if it wasn't Corey I didn't really give a damn.

I raised my hands above my head and slammed the center of the duct tape into my knees to free myself just as the agent had instructed. Then I unbound my legs and sat there for another hour or two until I finally removed my Samsung Galaxy S6 from my pocket. It had a feature that would allow me to set a text message to send at a future time. I decided I would use that feature.

I typed a five-word message to my mom and set it to send the following day. *Remember that I love you.*

Next, I typed in the address to Shawn's grandmother's old house and set it to send to Detective Davenport at the same time my mother would get her message.

I lay down beside Shawn. Grabbed the Beretta. Asked God to forgive me. Raised the gun to my head. And pulled the trigger.

Brandi

Any other time, Jasmine would have gotten back to me. She had me on pins and needles waiting for the scoop on what she found out about Corey and that Yvette chick.

"Yes. I would like to get this dress," I responded to the sales clerk. "This will be just perfect for the occasion."

"I hope you don't mind me asking, but who passed away?" The clerk questioned.

I couldn't do anything but laugh. "Funeral? I ain't going to no damn funeral--not yet," I boasted. "I'm going to a wedding. This black dress is perfect to celebrate such an affair. Don't you think?" I responded with a devious grin.

The clerk looked puzzled. She didn't respond at all. I couldn't blame her. If I had time, I would have probably shared with her the whole damn storyline, minus the part about how I helped two people get killed.

"Thank you for shopping with us," she said as she quickly handed me my dress and scurried away to help another customer.

As I walked out of the store, my phone rang. "Hey Jasmine! It's about time you called," I said. "I've been waiting."

Corey

It was the day of the wedding. I was nervous, happy, excited and scared. I still hadn't completely wrapped my mind around the fact that Joe-Joe was back. I thought back to the night of the incident with Mannie. I held Joe-Joe in my arms and begged him not to die on me until the ambulance arrived. His blood was all over my clothes. But if I had to be honest, that nigga *was* alive when I last saw him. He was riddled with bullet holes; I didn't think there was any way he would survive. But he was alive when he got in that ambulance. I guess I just assumed he died. Then when they had the funeral, I knew for sure. Or so I thought. Come to think of it though, my boy Tony did tell me that it was a closed casket funeral. I'm stunned.

Witness protection, though? Something was fishy about his story. What was he being protected from? Better yet, who was he being protected from? Witness protection is for snitches. My mind ran in circles. I wanted to figure out what was really going on with Joe-Joe, but I didn't want it to consume me on my wedding day. You know that ole saying "keep your friends close and your enemies closer"? Well, I asked Joe-Joe to be my best man. I needed to keep him on my hip.

My phone rang. I looked down and it was Felicia. My heart dropped. I didn't want to answer, but I told myself that I at least owed her the conversation. She'd held me down for so long. I loved her, but Yvette was the love of my life.

"Hello."

"Corey?" Her voice was shaky like she'd been crying.

"Hi Felicia. Listen, I'm sorry that..."

"Congratulations, Corey. I hope she makes you happy."

The line disconnected. She didn't call back. Neither did I. It was just easier to move on.

My phone rang again. This time it was a private number. I hit ignore. I was getting annoyed because I'd been getting blocked calls and hang ups for a few days. I just assumed it was Brandi. I had no desire to talk to her. I didn't owe her anything. I'd just talked to one of only two people I had an obligation to. The other one was about to be my wife.

I looked at the time. In less than four hours I was going to be a husband. I gathered my things and walked them down to my freshly painted Escalade. I had to meet my boys so we could pick up our tuxedos.

When I made it downstairs to the spot where my truck was parked, I noticed a bright yellow Mustang convertible screeching off. I couldn't believe my eyes. It was the fine ass chick with the dreds from the hotel. She'd been there the day someone scratched the letters D-A-D-D-Y. Now this time as she sped out the parking lot of my apartment building, even from a distance I saw the letters H-U-S-B-A-N-D scratched into the passenger side door of my ride.

Yvette

Who knew being a bride could be so stressful? I mean as little girls all our lives we dream of this day. The day we walk down the aisle in front of a host of friends and family from the arms of our father, right into the arms of our soon to be husband. It was crazy. I was excited to become a wife. But this day was stressing me completely out.

I'd been calling Jasmine over and over, but she wasn't answering. How could this be? My maid of honor was nowhere to be found. She'd been acting strange since the day she saw my diamond ring. But I chalked it up to her being busy and maybe even a little jealous.

I was initially apprehensive about asking her to be in the wedding. After all, she'd never formally been introduced to Corey so I wondered if she could truly execute her duties as my right hand in this ceremony. But my man told me that my family was his family and it wasn't specifically necessary for him to meet Jasmine before we wed. That's why I loved Corey. He was so supportive.

I called Jasmine once more. If she didn't answer this time, I was going to call my friend Candace to come through and scoop me. I didn't have but a few hours to get everything prepared and I couldn't make shit happen from this hotel.

When Jasmine didn't pick up, I left her a voicemail.

"Jasmine! Bitch, where the hell are you? If you don't get your dredheaded ass to this room to pick me up, I'm going to kill you! Call me ASAP!"

I disconnected the phone and dialed Candace immediately after. She said she could be at the hotel in less than an hour. I wasn't surprised. Candace had always been someone I could depend on. When I hung up with her, I packed up everything I would need and set it all by the door. Then I walked over to the hotel window and stared out hoping to see Jasmine's yellow Mustang pull up.

Brandi

Sitting in the rocker thinking about everything Corey had taken me through, I sniffed cocaine from the baby's blanket and cried most of the afternoon. It was the day of their wedding and I was devastated. It felt like the weight of the world was on my shoulders and it was too much to carry. I thought I wanted to know all about Yvette, but when Jasmine called and laid it all on the line, I really wished she hadn't told me anything at all. Hearing all the details hurt too badly. I hated Jasmine for telling me.

I wiped the tears from my eyes with the end of the baby blanket, then snorted another line of coke. I sat in that rocker for hours. Every time it seemed that I was coming around and getting used to the idea that there was no more me and Corey, I'd start crying again. It was a sad shame that everything had come down to this. But it is what it is and Corey was going to pay.

I picked up my cell, hit *67 to block my number, and called him again. I'd been doing it for days and he never picked up. I wonder if he knew it was me. I hoped he didn't, but in a way I hoped he did. His voicemail greeting picked up. I was tempted to leave a message. But I didn't. What good would it do? He'd made up his mind. A line was drawn in the sand. As far as I was concerned Corey waged war when he decided to marry Yvette's ugly ass.

I picked up my cell again. Only now, I checked the time. It was close. Time for me to get dressed for the wedding. I had no intention of being punctual. I wanted to arrive fashionably late. Just in time to hear the minister ask if anyone objected.

Yep! That would be me. And the little black dress I'd purchased was going to be perfect for the occasion.

Yvette

I couldn't believe it was finally happening. I was nervously talking to Candace. We were in the back of the church waiting for the ceremony to begin. Jasmine had stood me up. I'm not quite sure why, but I wasn't going to worry about it. Today was my wedding day. It had been a long time coming and nothing or no one was going to ruin it for me. Candace happily switched into the role of maid of honor and we proceeded as if Jasmine didn't exist. Honestly, I should have asked Candace to be my maid of honor first anyway. After all, she was the reason Corey and I met to begin with.

I unfolded the piece of paper I was holding that had my wedding vows handwritten on it. I'd written them weeks ago and had been practicing since then, but I still didn't quite have it down. I mean, I knew the words, but I wanted to recite them perfectly. I asked Candace to listen and tell me if it sounded corny.

"I take you to be my partner for life. I promise above all else to live in truth with you. And to communicate fully and fearlessly. I give you my hand and my heart as a sanctuary of warmth and peace and pledge my love, devotion, faith and honor as I join my life to yours."

I could hardly finish the last sentence before my eyes filled with tears. I looked up from the paper at Candace. She nodded her approval as tears streamed down her face as well.

"I love you friend. Your vows are perfect. Now we better stop all of this crying before we ruin our makeup."

Just as she said that, the wedding coordinator stuck her head in the door to let us know it was time.

"They're ready. The ceremony is about to begin."

Corey

I can't lie. I hate weddings. Men just do. Thugs do for sure. I wanted to marry Yvette but I wasn't standing at the altar in front of our friends and family looking all sappy because I wanted to. I did it because this is what she wanted and I wanted to make her happy. As I stood there waiting for her, tears threatened to fill my eyes. I took a deep breath and pressed my lips together. I had no intention of being that ultra-sensitive nigga who looked like a punk, crying on his wedding day. I could feel it. All eyes were on me. The crowd was waiting for me to break down. They were looking for their romantic love story. But I wasn't giving them that.

My mind raced. Was I ready? Was this really what I wanted to do? I mean, I loved Yvette, but was a brother truly ready to spend his entire life with just one piece of ass? That was funny. I tried not to laugh outwardly at myself. I didn't want to look crazy standing up at the altar laughing for what would seem like nothing to others. I told myself I was ready. Yvette was the woman I would give the rest of my life to.

My phone buzzed in my pocket. Sad shame that I almost answered it. It was just instinctive. But I didn't move a muscle. I let it vibrate. All of the important people in my life were sharing this moment with me. There was no one to answer for. My mind drifted off for a second to all the things that had happened up to this point. You know how people say in a near death experience their life flashes in front of them. Well, the events of the past year flashed in front of me. Meeting Yvette. The baby. Jail. Killing Shawn. Everything. I caught eyes with Joe-Joe. *Witness protection?* I wasn't too sure this nigga was supposed to be standing beside me on one of the most important days of my life, but I shrugged it off and kept it moving.

The sound of the organ playing the wedding march snapped me out of my thoughts. I looked up and my wife to be was walking through the double doors of the church auditorium. She looked angelic. That white dress clung to her body just right. She walked slowly, methodically down the aisle. Her dad held her tightly, like he didn't want to let her go. Next thing I knew, they stood before me. Her dad lifted her veil. She smiled. I smiled back. Then came those punk ass tears. I did everything I could not to cry, but it happened anyway. Her eyes widened. She smiled again. I mouthed the words "I love you".

We turned to face the minister. He began to speak. "Dearly beloved, we are gathered here today…"

Yvette beautifully recited the vows she'd personally written for this day. I knew every word verbatim. I'd heard her practice them over and over. And even though I knew everything she'd prepared, it still touched my heart. I cried again.

Then it was my turn. I froze. But eventually I got it out. I didn't write any vows. I just spoke from the heart.

"Yvette. You know me better than anyone else in this world and somehow still you manage to love me. You are my best friend and one true love. There is still a part of me today that cannot believe that I'm the one who gets to marry you…."

I paused. Everyone was waiting for me to continue. But I was done

"…and. That's it. That's all I got."

I laughed a little and the audience laughed too. Once we were completely through that part, the minister asked for the rings.

"But before we move forward with the ring ceremony, if anyone can show just cause why this couple cannot lawfully be joined together in matrimony, let them speak now or forever hold their peace…"

The doors to the church flung open as if someone had been standing on the other side waiting for the precise moment that the minister uttered those words. Sun rays from the outside made their way in. It was so bright; I put my hand up over my eyes to shield the light. Then I saw her. It was Brandi, in a form fitting black dress. My heart dropped. I couldn't believe she would show up here. I didn't know how to react. Joe-Joe thought quickly. He rushed down the aisle and grabbed Brandi forcefully by her arms back toward the double doors. But just as he was making an exit with her, in walked Detectives Davenport and Luis. They strolled up the walkway without regard to my wedding or my guests. And when they made it to me, Detective Luis spoke.

"Corey Wright. You have the right to remain silent…"

www.ingramcontent.com/pod-product-compliance
Lightning Source LLC
Chambersburg PA
CBHW071513170626
46811CB00007B/2847